SHEILA HETI is the author of eight books of fiction and nonfiction, including *How Should a Person Be?* which *New York* magazine deemed one of the "New Classics of the 21st century." She was named one of "The New Vanguard" by *The New York Times* book critics, who, along with a dozen other magazines and newspapers, chose *Motherhood* as a top book of 2018. Her books have been translated into twenty-one languages.

MOTHERHOOD

MOTHERHOOD

MOTHERHOOD

SHEILA HETI

A HOLT PAPERBACK

HENRY HOLT AND COMPANY

NEW YORK

MOTHERHOOD. Copyright © 2018 by Sheila Heti. All rights reserved. Printed in the United States of America. For information, address Henry Holt and Company, 120 Broadway, New York, N.Y. 10271.

www.henryholt.com

A Holt Paperback® and ⅓® are registered trademarks of Macmillan Publishing Group, LLC.

Grateful acknowledgment is made for permission to reprint from the following:
"The Cradle" (1872) by Berthe Morisot. "Jacob Wrestling with the Angel" (1865) by Alexandre-Louis Leloir. "Vision After the Sermon" (1888) by Paul Gauguin. Tarot cards from Shadowscapes © 2010 Stephanie Law. Reprinted with permission.
"Cocoon on the pokok" (2010) by Kerina Yin. "Dog on the train platform" © 2015 Helen Scarr. Used with permission. All additional images courtesy of the author.

Designed by Jennifer Griffiths

The Library of Congress has cataloged the hardcover edition as follows:

Names: Heti, Sheila, 1976– author.
Title: Motherhood / Sheila Heti.
Description: First edition. | New York : Henry Holt and Company, 2018.
Identifiers: LCCN 2017041243 (print) | LCCN 2017047816 (ebook) |
  ISBN 9781627790772 (hardcover) | ISBN 9781627790789 (ebook)
Subjects: LCSH: Motherhood—Fiction.
Classification: LCC PR9199.4.H48 (ebook) | LCC PR9199.4.H48 M68 2018 (print) |
  DDC 813/.6—dc23
LC record available at https://lccn.loc.gov/2017041243

ISBN: 978-1-250-21478-2 (trade paperback)

Our books may be purchased in bulk for promotional, educational, or business use. Please contact your local bookseller or the Macmillan Corporate and Premium Sales Department at 1-800-221-7945, extension 5442, or by email at MacmillanSpecialMarkets@macmillan.com.

Originally published in hardcover in 2018 by Henry Holt and Company

First Holt Paperbacks Edition 2023

Flipping three coins is a technique used by people who consult the *I Ching*, a divination system that originated in China over three thousand years ago. Kings used it in times of war, and regular people used it to help them with life problems. By flipping three coins six times, one of sixty-four states is revealed and a text elaborates their meaning. Confucius, one of the most important interpreters of the *I Ching*, said that if he had fifty years to spare, he would devote them to the book's study. The original text of the *I Ching* is poetic, dense, highly symbolic and intricately systematic, profoundly philosophical, cosmological in its sweep, and notoriously arcane.

In the pages that follow, three coins are used—a technique inspired by the *I Ching*, but not the actual *I Ching*, which is something different.

In this book, all results from the flipping of coins
result from the flipping of actual coins.

MOTHERHOOD

I often beheld the world at a great distance, or I didn't behold it at all. At every moment, birds passed by overhead that I did not see, clouds and bees, the rustling of breezes, the sun on my flesh. I lived only in the greyish, insensate world of my mind, where I tried to reason everything out and came to no conclusions. I wished to have the time to put together a world view, but there was never enough time, and also, those who had it, seemed to have had it from a very young age, they didn't begin it at forty. Literature, I knew, was the only thing that could be begun at forty. If you were forty, beginning it, you could be said to be young. In everything else, I was old, all the boats were far off, away from the shore, while I was still making my way to the shore, I hadn't even found my boat yet. The girl who was staying with us—she was twelve—made me see my own limitations as no one else had: my frailty, my obedience, my petty rebellions; most of all, my ignorance and sentimentality. When I entered the living room in the morning, half a hot dog was on the table. I called it a banana. Then I knew I was too old for this world, that she had quite naturally surpassed me, and would continue to. To transform the greyish and muddy landscape of my mind into a solid and concrete thing, utterly apart from me, indeed not me at all, was my only hope. I didn't know what this solid form would be, or what shape it would take. I only knew that I had to create a powerful monster, since I was such a weak one. I had to create a monster apart from me, that knew more than I knew, had a world view, and did not get such simple words wrong.

Flipping three coins on a desk. Two or three heads—yes. Two or three tails—no.

Is this book a good idea?

yes

Is the time to start it now?

yes

Here, in Toronto?

yes

So then there's nothing to be worried about?

yes

Yes, there's nothing to be worried about?

no

Should I be worried?

yes

What should I be worried about? My soul?

yes

Will reading help my soul?

yes

Will being quiet help my soul?

yes

Will this book help my soul?

yes

So then I'm doing everything right?

no

Am I handling my relationship wrong?

no

Am I wrong in ignoring the suffering of others?

no

Am I wrong in ignoring the political world?

no

Am I wrong in not being grateful for the life I have?

yes

And the things I can do with it, having this time and prosperity?

no

Having my particular being?

yes

Is the time for worrying about my particular being over?

yes

Is this the time to begin thinking about *the soul of time*?

yes

Do I have everything I need to begin?

yes

Should I start at the beginning and move straight through to the end?

no

Should I do whatever I feel like, then stitch it all together later?

no

Should I start at the beginning, not knowing what will come next?

yes

Is this conversation the beginning?

yes

How about those rolls of colored tape Erica bought me, sitting over there. Should I use them somehow?

no

Should I just let them sit there and look at them?

no

Should I give them back to her?

no

Should I hide them from sight?

yes

In the cupboard?

yes.

It's going to be so hard not thinking about myself, but rather thinking about *the soul of time.* I have so little practice thinking about *the soul of time*, and so much practice thinking about myself.

But nothing is easy at the start. The phrase *the soul of time* has been with me since Erica and I took that trip to New York over New Year's Eve several months ago. It was in my head shortly before that trip, too. I remember explaining it to her in detail on the subway platform. We were staying at Teresa and Walter's apartment. They were out of town, visiting family over Christmas. I threw up that night, drunk, in their toilet. But this was much earlier in the day. Was it December 31?

no

Funny, I don't remember it being cold, and I don't remember wearing a coat. Was it January 1?

no

December 30?

no

Was it some other trip entirely?

yes

I don't think it was. I was explaining to Erica about *the soul of time*, about how either we as individuals have no souls, but experience a sort of collective soul that either belongs to time or *is* time, or that our lives—*we*—are time's soul. I wasn't entirely clear on which one it was. The idea was in its infancy, and still is today. She got very excited, while I found the idea that my soul was not my possession very comforting—that either my life was an expression of time's soul, or that my soul was time. I don't know if I'm getting it right. Am I?

no

No, no. I hope to better understand what I meant on the subway platform, and what so excited my dear friend Erica. This will be my stated purpose, my design or agenda, in writing this—to

understand what it means, *the soul of time*, or to explain it to myself.
Is that a good premise for this book?

no

Is it too narrow?

yes

Can *the soul of time* be involved?

no

Am I allowed to betray you?

yes

Then that's definitely partly what this book will be about.
Maybe I shouldn't have said that I wanted *to explain it to myself*
but rather *explain it to other people*. Is that better?

no

To *embody it* rather than *explain it*?

yes

I have a headache. I'm so tired. I shouldn't have taken that nap.
But if I hadn't taken that nap, I would be in an even worse mood
than I am right now, right?

no.

~

Today I cried as Miles was leaving the house. When he asked
why, I said it was because I had *nothing to do*. He said, *You're a
writer. You have the* Bonjour Philippine *book, you have the* I Ching
book—you have the Simone Weil *book. Why don't you work on one
of those?* He hesitated before bringing up the Simone Weil
book, because it was his idea that I write about the ideas of
Simone Weil, and right after he said it, several weeks ago, both

he and I became uncomfortable—that he should suggest a book idea to me. I rejected it outright, to his face, but around noon I started work on a book about Simone Weil. Miles texted me that afternoon to see if I was feeling better, and called me several hours later to ask the same thing. It's really him I should be worried about, not him who should be worried about me, because he is the one who just started working and has no time to study, right?

no

It's fair for both of us to be concerned about each other?

yes

I beat myself up over everything.

~

Around noon today, I took a drive in the country with my father. I was trying to decide whether to take a three-week trip to New York in June. Teresa had told me that she and Walter would be heading out of town, and that their apartment would be free if I wanted it. After much debating over what to do, I decided to make the choice that would make me feel better and warmer inside right now, and that was to stay here. After the drive, I came home and took a nap and woke up with a good feeling. I sat on the purple couch in the bedroom and just thought. I have for so long been putting off starting a new book, but now that Miles has begun working long hours, the choice has presented itself: to make a change and run off to New York and have fun, or to *be a writer* as he put it—as he reminded me that I am. I wanted to tell him that I'm not the sort of writer who sits in her room and writes, but I did not. I remember how the other day he said that once a writer starts to have *an interesting life* their writing always suffers. My reply to him was, *You just don't want me to have an interesting life!* Does that continue to ring in his ears?

yes

Did it hurt his feelings?

yes

Will he one day just forget about it?

no

Must I apologize for it tonight?

yes.

~

Although Miles and I had been having a nice night, I apologized to him for that comment and told him I was not going to go to New York to stay in Teresa and Walter's apartment for three weeks. He said, *I don't relate to these values you always come back from New York with.* I love him. He just refilled the water in the vase with the lilacs, which he bought for me last week. They were dying, the lilacs on my desk, and I hadn't even noticed. Now the ice cream truck outside is playing its sad song, and I'm a little drunk from the wine I had earlier this evening. I'm feeling all right. Does it really matter how I'm feeling?

no

No, no. I didn't think so. So many feelings in a day. It's clearly not the rudder—not the oracle—not the thing you should steer your life by, not the map. Though there is always that temptation. What's a better thing to steer your life by? Your values?

yes

Your plans for the future?

no

Your artistic goals?

no

The things the people around you need—I mean, the things the people you love need?

yes

Security?

no

Adventure?

no

Whatever seems to confer soul, depth and development?

no

Whatever seems to bring happiness?

yes

So your values, happiness and the things the people around you need. Those are the things by which you should steer your life.

My mother cried for forty days and forty nights. As long as I have known her, I have known her to cry. I used to think that I would grow up to be a different sort of woman, that I would not cry, and that I would solve the problem of her crying. She could never tell me what was wrong except to say, *I'm tired*. Could it be that she was always tired? I wondered, when I was little, *Doesn't she know she's unhappy?* I thought the worst thing in the world would be to be unhappy, but not to know it. As I grew older, I compulsively checked myself for signs that I was unhappy. Then I grew unhappy, too. I grew filled up with tears.

All through my childhood, I felt I had done something wrong. I searched my every gesture, my words, the way I sat upon a chair. What was I doing to make her cry? A child thinks she is the cause of even the stars in the sky, so of course my mother's crying was all about me. Why had I been born to cause her pain? Since I had caused it, I wanted to take it away. But I was too little. I didn't even know how to spell my own name. Knowing so little, how could I have understood a single thing about her suffering? I still don't understand. No child, through her own will, can pull a mother out of her suffering, and as an adult, I have been very busy. I have been busy writing. My mother often says, *You are free*. Perhaps I am. I can do what I like. So I will stop her from crying. Once I am finished writing this book, neither one of us will ever cry again.

This will be a book to prevent future tears—to prevent me and my mother from crying. It can be called a success if, after reading it, my mother stops crying for good. I know it's not the job of a child to stop her mother from crying, but I'm not a child anymore. I'm a writer. The change I have undergone, from child to writer, gives me powers—I mean that magical powers are not far from my hand. If I am a good enough writer, perhaps I can stop her from crying. Perhaps I can figure out why she is crying, and why I cry, too, and I can heal us both with my words.

~

Is attention soul? If I pay attention to my mother's sorrow, does that give it soul? If I pay attention to her unhappiness— if I put it into words, transform it, and make it into something new—can I be like the alchemists, turning lead into gold? If I sell this book, I will get back gold in return. That's a kind of alchemy. The philosophers wanted to turn dark matter into gold, and I want to turn my mother's sadness into gold. When the gold comes in, I will go to my mother's doorstep, and I will hand it to her and say: *Here is your sadness, turned into gold.*

Should the title of this book be *The Soul of Time*?

yes

Should it have a subtitle?

no

It's relaxing to have a title, whether or not it's a good one. Is it a good one?

no

No, but that's the way it's going to be?

yes

I suppose it doesn't much matter, in the general scope of things. Of course, it might matter a lot to *me* whether the title of this book is a good or bad one, because I am the one responsible, and I will be the one to blame. The focus will be on me, and the judgement will come down on *my* poor taste. But for the world, whether one book has a good title or bad one doesn't much matter, so why should I concern myself with it? Does this *book* have to be any good at all?

no

Because it will never be published, because no one will ever see it?

yes

What's the point of writing something that no one will ever read? I forget who said that a work of art does not exist without an audience—that it's not enough for it to be made. Is it wrong to have an audience in mind when setting out on a work of art?

yes

Should you simply be trying to have an experience?

no

Does one do it for the non-audience that is God?

yes

To bring glory to the world?

no

Out of gratitude for being made alive?

yes

And because art is what humans do?

yes

Are my insecurities going to ruin my relationship?

yes

Is there anything I can do about it?

yes

Will it take a long time?

yes

Will our relationship be over by the time I have overcome them?

yes

Is there any good in that?

yes

Good in it for both of us?

yes

Miles is making us dinner right now. Is the more important thing than writing this to go into the kitchen and be with him there?

yes

All right. I'm going.

~

Now I'm sitting on our bed, with the cicadas humming outside. Miles is at the corner store. I have to return to the question I asked before dinner, *Will our relationship be over by the time I have overcome my insecurities?* I never considered, when I was asking it, that our relationship would be over by the time I overcame my insecurities because we only overcome our insecurities in death. Is that what you meant? That I will only overcome my insecurities in death, and that our love and relationship will last till my death?

yes

Oh good! I feel so good. Everything feels a million times better than it did yesterday. I'm glad I'm not going to New York to stay in Teresa and Walter's apartment. It feels so much richer, fuller, and more alive to stay here.

Last night, I had a vivid dream, a wild dream of being with my son, who was five or so. I spent so much of the dream staring into his face. I knew it was him, knew it was a dream, and kept wanting to write it down—that this was happening; that I was encountering the face of my future son. It was clearly my son with Miles. The boy had slightly darker skin than Miles or me, and an intelligent, sensitive face. At one point, I was crying and tears were running down my face from sorrow; the boy was sitting on a windowsill in the kitchen, watching me, and I could tell he was overwhelmed by my adult feelings. I saw that I should not be putting so much of my emotional life on him; that it was too big a burden to bear. He seemed really delicate and lovely. I loved him, but I also felt like the love was not as I imagined it would be; it was not as deep to the core as I thought it would feel, I don't know why. I felt a little bit distant from him, a little bit alienated. But I loved looking at his face and into his eyes. I said to myself, *I can't believe I'm seeing the face of my future son!* I would love to have a child like that. He was slender and good.

I woke from the dream in the middle of the night, disgusted and horrified with how I have been living. For a woman nearing forty, earning not enough money, renting an apartment infested with mice, with no savings, no children, divorced, and still living in the city of her birth, it seemed I had not *thought* as my father advised me to do ten years ago, after my marriage ended: *Next time—THINK.* I saw I had not thought, but continued to let myself be whipped about in the waves of life, building nothing.

~

Miles has said that the decision is mine—he doesn't want a child apart from the one he had, quite by accident, when he was young, who lives in another country with her mother, and stays with us on holidays and half the summer. *It's a risk*, he says, his daughter is lovely, but you never know what you're going to get. If I want a child, we can have one, he said, *but you have to be sure.*

~

Whether I want kids is a secret I keep from myself—it is the greatest secret I keep from myself.

The thing to do when you're feeling ambivalent is to wait. But for how long? Next week I'll be thirty-seven. Time is running short on making certain decisions. How can we know how it will go for us, us ambivalent women of thirty-seven? On the one hand, the joy of children. On the other hand, the misery of them. On the one hand, the freedom of not having children. On the other hand, the loss of never having had them—but what is there to lose? The love, the child, and all those motherly feelings that the mothers speak about in such an enticing way, as though a child is something to have, not something to do. The doing is what seems hard. The having seems marvellous. But one doesn't have a child, one does it. I know I have more than most mothers. But I also have less. In a way, I have nothing at all. But I like that and think I do not want a child.

Yesterday I talked on the phone with Teresa, who is about fifty years old. I said that it seemed like other people were suddenly ahead of me with their marriages, their houses, their children, their savings. She said that when a person has those feelings, they need to look more closely at what their actual values are. We have to live our values. Often people are streamed into the conventional life—the life there's so much pressure to live. But how can there only be one path that's legitimate? She says this path is often not even right for many of the people who wind up living it. They become forty-five, fifty, then they hit a wall. *It's easy to bob along the surface,* she said. *But only for so long.*

~

Do I want children because I want to be admired as the admirable sort of woman who has children? Because I want to be seen as a normal sort of woman, or because I want to be the best kind of woman, a woman with not only work, but the desire and ability to nurture, a body that can make babies, and someone who another person wants to make babies with? Do I want a child to show myself to be the (normal) sort of woman who wants and ultimately has a child?

The feeling of not wanting children is the feeling of not wanting to be someone's idea of me. Parents have something greater than I'll ever have, but I don't want it, even if it's so great, even if in a sense they've won the prize, or grabbed the golden ring, which is genetic relief—relief at having procreated; success in the biological sense, which on some days seems like the only sense that matters. And they have social success, too.

There is a kind of sadness in not wanting the things that give so many other people their life's meaning. There can be sadness at not living out a more universal story—the supposed life cycle—how out of one life cycle another cycle is supposed to come. But when out of your life, no new cycle comes, what does that feel like? It feels like nothing. Yet there is a bit of a let-down feeling when the great things that happen in the lives of others—you don't actually want those things for yourself.

It is so hard to conceive of making art without an audience who will eventually see it. I know we make art because we're humans, and that's what humans do, for the sake of God. But will *God* ever see it?

no

Is that because art *is* God?

no

Is it because art exists in the house of God, but God doesn't pay attention to what's in God's home?

yes

Is art at home in the world?

yes

Is art a living thing—while one is making it, that is? As living as anything else we call living?

yes

Is it as living when it is bound in a book or hung on a wall?

yes

Then can a woman who makes books be let off the hook by the universe for not making the living thing we call babies?

yes

Oh good! I feel so guilty about it sometimes, thinking it's what I *should* do, because I always think that animals are happiest when they live out their instincts. Maybe not happiest, but feel most alive. Yet making art makes me feel alive, and taking care of others doesn't make me feel as alive. Maybe I have to think about myself less as a woman with this woman's special task, and more as an individual with her own special task—not put *woman* before my individuality. Is that right?

no

Is it that making babies is *not* a woman's special task?

yes

I should not be asking questions in the negative. *Is* it her special task?

yes

Yes, but the universe lets women who make art but don't make babies, off the hook? Does the universe mind if women who *don't* make art choose not to make babies?

yes

Are these women punished?

yes

By not experiencing the mystery and joy?

yes

In any other way?

yes

By not passing on their genes?

yes

But I don't care about passing on my genes! Can't one pass on one's genes through art?

yes

Do *men* who don't procreate receive punishment from the universe?

no

Do they receive punishment for neglecting other tasks one typically associates with maleness?

no

Men escape all damnation and can do whatever they want?

no

Perhaps their punishment comes not from the universe but from society?

yes

Does it take the form of ridicule?

yes

From women?

no

From other men?

yes

And is their suffering as great as the suffering of these women at the hands of the universe?

yes

Well, I guess that seems fair.

yes.

~

Yesterday, Erica, whose first baby is due any week now, sent me a painting by Berthe Morisot. She said, *This painting reminds me of you. It's what I think you'd look like if you had a child.* I wrote her back saying that the woman in the painting looked a little bored, but she replied saying that the woman was *interested* in her sleeping baby, and felt I would be, too. I had interpreted the woman's hand as having been placed on the edge of the bassinet kind of carelessly, without a thought. But Erica said she felt the hand was laid over the edge of the crib *tenderly and protectively.*

That does seem good—to lay your hand on reality. To move away from the distortions of your mind and feel what actually is.

~

This afternoon, I went to my doctor. She did a check-up, then asked me questions about my life, including what sort of contraception Miles and I were using. I grew embarrassed, admitting the truth: pulling out. It was what I had used with almost every man. *What if you get pregnant? Would you be okay with that?* I tried to answer in an easy way, but soon my sentences got twisted up.

After the appointment, I walked in the streets and called Teresa. I brought up my worries over paths not taken, and she said everyone had those, but often when you looked back on your life, you saw that the choices you made and the paths you went down were the right ones. She said it wasn't a matter of choosing one life over another, but being sensitive to the life that wants to be lived through you. You need tension in order to create something—the sand in the pearl. She said my questioning and doubts were the sand. She said they were good and forced me to live with integrity, to interrogate what was important to me, and so to live the meaning of my life, rather than resort to convention.

Then to try and discover and live my values, even if it may not seem like I'm moving forward in my life, while my friends appear to be moving forward in theirs—ticking off all the boxes. Ask only whether you are living your values, not whether the boxes are ticked.

After our call, I realized the thing I always do: I try to imagine different futures for myself, what I would most like to occur. I don't know why I do this, when any of the things I've hoped for—whenever I have actually got them—are nothing like what I imagined they'd be. Then why don't I spend time acclimating myself to what actually occurred? Why not make peace with the way things are, given what I know about life from actually living? Instead I spin fantasies, when the only happiness I have ever known has occurred without my design.

~

Your idea about what your life is about, or should be like, occurs even before your life has had a chance to unfold. So much time that hasn't had the opportunity to present itself, you spend in efforts trying to make the space ahead fill in exactly the way you hope it might. So what is the point in having that time? Of being in it at all? Why don't you just die when a sufficiently pleasing idea about what your life ought to look like materializes in your mind?

The reason we don't just kill ourselves when we have figured out what we want our lives to look like is because we actually want to experience things. But what happens when things we thought we wanted to experience *don't* occur? Or when something we didn't think we wanted to experience *does*? What's the point in living all that other stuff, the stuff we never wanted, the stuff we didn't choose?

Since life rarely accords to our expectations, why bother expecting anything at all? Wouldn't it be better not to plan ahead? But that seems crazy, too, because planning and desiring sometimes works. Even if it doesn't work, it still gets us somewhere. Or at least it seems like if we didn't desire and plan, we'd be stuck in one place.

It is often said that whether or not to have children is the biggest decision a person can make. That may be true, but it also doesn't mean anything. A decision happens in the private mind of one. It is not an action. For things to happen in a life, other people must participate. You have to will it. Many things have to collaborate. Life itself has to will it. A decision in the mind is pretty small. It doesn't make babies.

If a decision in the mind doesn't make babies, why do I spend so much time thinking about it? We are judged by what happens to us as though our deciding made it happen. A lot of time is wasted in thinking about whether to have a child, when the thinking is such a small part of it, and when there is little enough time to think about things that actually bring meaning. Which are what?

Nobody completely expected it to go the way it went—their life. Nobody is completely happy with the way things turned out for them. But most people manage to find some pleasure in it anyway.

~

A friend of mine who was dating a man, quite early on in their fucking *heard the sound* and agreed to go ahead. She told him to come inside her. Then she got pregnant, and she chose to break up with him, but they remained friends. She found a boyfriend who she wanted to raise the child with, and the father takes the kid on weekends. They all love the boy and everything seems fine. What a way to live! To respond to the call and, once that's done, make the practical decisions and make them well.

I also heard the sound last August, deeply in my soul. I never wanted a child as much as I did that month. I remember sitting on the lakeside dock of my friend's mother's cottage, telling her of my desire—but not telling Miles, for he had only started articling at a criminal defence firm a month before, and it didn't seem fair to bring it up with him then. The timing wasn't right. Nine months later, four of my friends gave birth. What was the sound we all heard that August?

~

When I was younger, I told myself that if I was ever going to have a child, it would only happen if I accidentally became pregnant. Well, I did accidentally become pregnant, and I decided not to keep it.

I was twenty-one at the time, and switching to the birth control pill. The moment I discovered I was pregnant, I decided I would have an abortion. There was no gap between finding out and knowing what I wanted to do.

The doctor who examined me advised me to keep the baby. He showed me the sonogram, even though I didn't want to see it. He told me it was too early to get an abortion. Because it was possible that I could miscarry, he said it would be wrong to do it now. He joked that I should have the baby and give it to him; he said I could come over to his house with bags of milk every week. It wasn't until I left his office that I realized what he meant: milk that would come from my breasts.

I spent the days before my next appointment doing nothing but waiting for my abortion—smoking pot, eating candies and chocolate and chips, drinking and smoking too much, as if to poison the little thing that was growing inside me, that was making me nauseous all day.

Only today, as I'm writing this, does it occur to me that he was lying; he wanted me to change my mind. You don't have to wait for an abortion. But I was too young then, and too all alone, to see it.

~

Why are we still having children? Why was it important for that doctor that I did? A woman must have children because she must be occupied. When I think of all the people who want to forbid abortions, it seems it can only mean one thing—not that they want this new person in the world, but that they want that woman to be doing the work of child-rearing more than they want her to be doing anything else. There is something threatening about a woman who is not occupied with children. There is something at-loose-ends feeling about such a woman. What is she going to do instead? What sort of trouble will she make?

This afternoon, I went to see my friend Mairon in her new home. She held her baby on her lap like he was a delicate toy. She said, *Oh—I just realized! One day you will call me and tell me you're pregnant!* She said I seemed very fertile—as if becoming a mother had made her psychic, as if she could gauge someone's fertility by being near them.

She said the first time she saw her son, she thought, *Oh my god, I almost didn't do this!* She hadn't always wanted a child—in fact, up until the moment the baby came out, she didn't know whether she did. Her husband had proposed it as a kind of game—take the plunge with him!—and she agreed.

She lit up like a sunbeam when she learned that Miles and I were still together. She said, *One man is no better than the next—unless he beats you, gambles, cheats or drinks, it'll be the same issues with any other man that you have with Miles.* She explained that she and her husband had recently decided that they would not get divorced.

How interesting, I said, *that it's a separate decision from the decision to get married.*

It is, she said. *All we fight about anymore is money. We leave the trivial stuff alone.*

Every particle in her wanted me to settle down and make babies. She admitted it, too—that she wanted all of her friends

33

to be married off with babies, like she was. I agreed that it did seem like an adventure, and it was flattering to be told, as she did, *You'd be very good at it.*

Is there some part of me that knows whether or not I'll have a baby? Will I *do my time,* as Mairon put it, like how the men once did their time in the army? Will I marry Miles, then promise not to divorce him, and never have an *avant-garde life*? Mairon chided me when I said this was what I wanted: *That's making too much of an intellectual puzzle out of it. That's not the truth. That's not what life is. There is no such thing as an avant-garde life.*

As I was leaving her house, I ran into a former professor of mine. It was in her Classics course years ago that Mairon and I met. She was on her way up the steps to visit the baby, and we stopped to say hello. I told her about my visit, and about what Mairon wanted for my life. She said, *Please, don't have children.* The professor had a daughter who was thirty-five. I knew she was trying to save me from drudgery and pain. I said, *But wasn't having a daughter the greatest experience of your life?* She paused for a moment, then admitted it was.

~

What to do about these dangerous and beautiful sirens, like Mairon, whose songs, though irresistibly sweet, are no less sad than sweet? The term *siren song* refers to an appeal that is hard to resist, but that, if heeded, will bring the one who heeds it to a very bad end. Their song takes effect at midday, in a windless calm, and lulls the soul and body into a fatal lethargy—the beginning of one's corruption.

Then resist like the monks who resist lying with women—no matter how good it would make them feel. Sing your songs more beautifully to yourself than the tempting mothers sing them. Sing your songs so beautifully, for the charms of their music, and the songs they sing, will soon make you forget your native land.

~

Yesterday, Miles and I had a long conversation about women artists having children. He said many things about why it was so made up, the joys of parenting, and that really it's like tilling the field. And why should people with other work to do also till the field? Why should everyone have to? He went on to say what a lot of time it was, and that it sort of blows your load, parenting, because it's the perfect job—it's very hard but only *you* can do it. *And isn't making art like that?* he asked. If you can get that existential satisfaction from parenthood, would you feel as much desire to make art? He said that one can either be a great artist and a mediocre parent, or the reverse, but not great at both, because both art and parenthood take all of one's time and attention. These are the sort of thoughts I always try to push from my mind. It caused me some sadness to hear him talk this way, but I have also never really understood myself to be a mother, even if in moments I thought I could be. He says we do not have the money, we'd have to move, change everything. *We're not made—cut to the cloth—to have normal lives.* Finally, he was talking about how cultures have always held places for those who don't want children: in the clergy—nuns and priests; scholars and artists. As for the vow of chastity demanded by the church, he thought ultimately it had to do with the fact that those given over to difficult spiritual work should not have to be chasing children around, and that societies feel these people contribute in other ways and give them a pass. All morning I felt a kind of coldness in my chest towards him. Why must I be one of the people he's talking about?

I spoke about not having children as a *sacrifice,* and he said, *but what are you sacrificing?* I listened to him very carefully, then remembered the sensation I had of utter deepening—once, when we were in the kitchen; about how if I stayed with him, that's how deep I would go into writing and life, into the darkest corners of myself and the earth.

Then perhaps I should be grateful if he doesn't want us to have a child. In a sense, I should be grateful.

~

Before going to bed tonight, Miles and I argued about money. Who should pay for what, and how—that is what started the fight. He is in debt from law school, and sends money away for his child, while I have never been in debt, having worked all the way through university—my fear of debt being so great. I have never put my money together with a man, or taken money from a boyfriend before, or ever supported a man, or been supported by one, either. I have so many awful memories of my parents arguing about money, and in trying to keep my money separate, it was fights like these I strove to avoid.

~

Last night, I dreamed Miles broke up with me on a bus, and as soon as he did it, he put his arm around a small, demure, brunette young woman who was sitting beside him. I was devastated that I had acted in such a way—emotional, difficult—as to make him want to leave me. But I kind of wanted to break up, too, and I had a hard time explaining to him that I was the way I was—sensitive, difficult—as a result of who *he* was; that I wouldn't be this way with another man.

Eventually my jealousy will fade, I hope. Miles has said he thinks the only thing worth being in this world is a decent person with courage, and that he has never *done that*—lied to a woman or deceived her. I have only two choices: to trust him or be suspicious of him; to believe in him or to doubt. Then I ought to make the choice to trust him, because what good does it do me to be suspicious or to doubt? That is causing myself pain in advance of any real pain.

I have to ask, am I like those pale, brittle women writers who never leave the house, who don't have kids, and who always kind of fascinated and horrified me?

yes

Is there anything I can do to avoid being that way?

no

Is there real shame in being that way?

yes

Is *that way* basically selfish?

yes

And not as connected to the life force as other women, being so shut up in my thoughts and my head?

yes

Is there a male equivalent to this, well, barrenness?

no

Is there a romantic female figure that equals those male, romantic, artistic figures?

yes

Women artists with children?

yes

If I have children, will I be like those women?

no

Would I have to give up writing in order to be?

yes

And dedicate my life to a man?

yes

To Miles?

no

To my father?

yes

Will dedicating my life to my father and giving up writing make me into a romantic female figure?

yes

Should I move in with him now?

yes

But wouldn't that make me unhappy?

yes

Wouldn't I be happier here?

yes

Does it matter whether a person is a romantic figure or not?

no.

~

When I moved out of my parents' house the week after high school ended, my mother gave up raising me. She says she should have given up long before. I remember the first time she and my father visited me in the little room I had rented. It was such a depressing little room, with a tiny bathroom attached. But for me, it was absolute heaven. My mother stood there crying, hurt. Why had I left our family, and why had I left our beautiful home, to live in this lonely little room, with only a hot plate, no kitchen, and just enough room for a bed and a desk?

My mother also left home when she was seventeen—to attend medical school in the nearest town. But she didn't see my moving out as a similar act to hers—moving out in order to start my life and write, both of us ready to work as soon as we could, eager to work forever. My mother works hard, and I work hard, too. I took the lesson of hard work from her. That is what a mother does: she sits in her room and works hard.

When I was younger, thinking about whether I wanted children, I always came back to this formula: if no one had told me anything about the world, I would have invented boyfriends. I would have invented sex, friendships, art. I would not have invented child-rearing. I would have had to invent all those other things to fulfil real longings in me, but if no one had ever told me that a person could create a person, and raise them into a citizen, it wouldn't have occurred to me as something to do. In fact, it would have sounded like a task to very much avoid.

Not that it really matters, the question of what my *authentic* or original desire might be. I know a person can enjoy things they never thought they would, and regret terribly things they wanted very much, or can come to want things they didn't want before.

~

What I need is so small: to eradicate any sentimentality from my feelings and to look at what is. Today, I defined *sentimental* to myself as *a feeling about the idea of a feeling*. And it seemed to me that my inclinations towards motherhood had a lot to with *the idea of a feeling* about motherhood.

It's like the story my religious cousin told me when we were at her home for Shabbat dinner—of the girl who made chicken the way her mother did, which was the way *her* mother did: always tying the chicken legs together before putting it in the pot. When the girl asked her mother why she tied the legs together, her mother said, *That's the way my mother did it.* When the girl asked her grandmother why she did it that way, her grandmother said, *That's how my mother did it.* When she asked her great-grandmother why it was important to tie the chicken legs together, the woman replied, *That's the only way it would fit in my pot.*

I think that is how childbearing feels to me: a once-necessary, now sentimental gesture.

~

There is a feeling I have of life standing by, twiddling its thumbs, waiting for me to have a child. I have sensed it creeping over my skin—the sensation of life tapping its foot, waiting for me to give birth to a child who could only be given birth to through me. Sometimes I feel there's a specific human life I'm denying—actively and selfishly denying—if I don't have a baby. I don't know where this idea comes from, or if every woman feels it, or if it's something from the past—from a historical event that happened when I had my abortion. Someone was being grown and I prevented that life from being. Yet I think of it, strangely, as a present-tense issue: *there's someone I'm not letting be born,* or a future-tense issue: *there's someone I won't let be born.*

Is there a part of me that thinks I can return to that life—re-animate the specific human life I ended? The same way it can be that for years after a break-up, you project yourself back before the break-up occurred, and live in the relationship as though it's still going on, fantasizing, *Maybe I can un-break their heart and bring us back together again.*

What should I do about the soul I blew the life out from, like blowing out a candle on a birthday cake? The Jewish religion says it's not a child until it's two-thirds out of the woman's body—until the head has completely emerged. I have a feeling like if I open my mouth too wide, a baby will pop out, like something I didn't want to say—I might slip up and say the unsayable thing. A baby's right there, building up at the back of my throat, a self that wants to come through me—not necessarily even *my child*—I don't even feel this child wants to be raised by me, only that I'm the vessel through which it must come. Should I do it? Let this thing be born—not for me, not for Miles, but just for that single, solitary soul?

If I accept the idea that there is a creature waiting to be born through me, and it's not some vague guilt about my abortion, then I become calm. Then it seems like the main thing about motherhood is letting another creature come through you, whose life is entirely its own. A child is not a combination of you and your partner, but a reality all its own, separate and unique—a distinct point of consciousness in the world. I don't think this was something I ever felt—that my body, my life, belonged to *me*.

~

This evening, Miles came into my study where I was writing— he had been putting the laundry together, and he said to me, *Why don't you write a book about motherhood? Since you're thinking about it so much. And talking about it with everyone you meet.* Then he returned to cleaning up. It's true. Lately I *have* been asking everybody, *Do you want to have kids?* Every conversation I get into with anyone, he has seen me turn in this direction.

Does your mother know the exact moment she became pregnant? The moment he entered my study and said that, I felt the first stirrings of new life. I knew there would be no turning back.

What kind of creature is gestating in me, that is half me and half him? What is this creature that is half the creation of a writer, and half the creation of a criminal defence lawyer? Of course, a woman will always be made to feel like a criminal, whatever choice she makes, however hard she tries. Mothers feel like criminals. Non-mothers do, too. So this creature, which is half me, half him, will be in part a written defence. Like Miles, it will want to help, to stick up for the accused. As his colleague once said to me of the work they do, *There are only two people on the side of the accused—his mother and his lawyer.*

NEW YORK

This afternoon, a psychic lady—a spiritual healer or fraud—stopped me on the street as I stood in the West Village, window-shopping after an interview. The interview had been conducted by a reporter who was writing for a 'things to do in New York' website, who was going to mention my reading that night.

I was standing in the sunny street, looking at puppies in the window of a shop, when an older woman stopped me and showed me the goosebumps on her arm—told me to touch them. Then she pulled me over to a bench on the other side of the street. Money didn't come up till later. Meanwhile, she could see it in my eyes—whatever it was she saw—that the Lord on high destined us to meet. The angel Gabriel was perched on her right shoulder, and the angel Michael was perched on her left (she told me, touching them).

She said my three colors were lavender, turquoise and silver, and that I should write with my left hand, because my power is on the left side of my body, which is where God has put my femininity. She asked me to point out the hand I write with, and I of course put out both my hands. But from now on I will write with my left hand, slowly and awkwardly, in a white notebook, as I'm doing now.

Do I have a gullible face? I must have. A hundred and forty dollars I gave her!—as she stood behind me at the ATM. But I justified it to myself by saying, *It cost less than a therapy session—and this was better than that.*

She asked me to make three wishes, but I could not. I cannot make wishes right now. I know that whatever you wish for has its dark side, too. But it was not so hard to come up with three questions, so I asked if I could provide her with three questions instead. She said *yes*. First I asked her how long it would take me to finish this book, and she closed her eyes and asked God (if it was God, but maybe it was the angels) and the answer was that I would write it *in days and weeks and months and years*, and that the book would lead me, but that eventually it would be done, and it would be my number one bestseller. She pointed out that I have to remember how many people have the same problems I do. The only reason I brought up the book is because she brought up the strength of my mother and grandmother, saying they had been the backbones of their families.

My second question was, *Why am I so sad?* She squeezed her eyes shut, then revealed that a man and a woman had put a curse on me, my mother, and her mother, while my mother was pregnant with me. She looked a little deeper into the unknown, then said, appearing to almost vomit in her mouth, *It's worse than I thought.* I asked if the people were alive or dead, and she said they were dead, but that only made the curse stronger. She put her hand on my belly and told me I was fertile—my machinery worked—but later she admitted that I had pre-cancerous cells in my womb.

She had me squeeze her finger three times hard *(harder—I can take it)* and push like I was pushing out a baby to reverse the curse (and, I think, the cancer). I repeated after she said it, *evil be out! evil be out! evil be out!* Then she said, *I see the head!* (she'd had me uncross my legs) and with the final push, I saw the whole thing come out, too.

At this point we talked about Miles, and she said we would be together the rest of our lives. She saw two girls for us. I would carry them nine months—*to full term, not preemie.* I said he was a noble man and she said I was a noble woman. I said, *Do you want to see a picture of him?* She said, *Thank you. I do!* I showed her his picture on my phone—us smiling in bed together.

She saw that he was honest and true. *It's good*, she said. *He loves you and wants to take care of you.* She gave me a little bag of stones in blue velvet to illustrate this, and made me cup it in my hands: *You can trust your life in his hands. And he can trust his life in yours.* Tears came into my eyes when she said we'd stay together. *A man like this doesn't grow on trees. Take it one day at a time.*

She said my task in life was to speak for the people who could not—and something about the four corners of the world—that my married name would be remembered, and my maiden name would be, too.

I had one final question: Should I live in Toronto, where I feel more at home, or in New York, which feels so free? She thought and said, *You will remain in Toronto until you finish your book, then you will move here.*

But what about Miles? You said we would be together forever. I was thinking about Miles's job, and how he cannot move. She said that Miles would move with me.

It was the best psychic reading I have ever had.

The next morning, before I flew home, I had breakfast with a young editor from an intellectual magazine. The restaurant was down a short flight of stairs. It was dark inside with round marble tables, cloth napkins, and a handwritten menu with only six items, all of them perfect.

What do we need to know about a person in order to like them? Before she wrapped her leftover buttered toast inside a paper napkin, I didn't know whether I liked her or not. Then, when she wrapped up her toast in the napkin, I suddenly loved her. Before she wrapped up her toast, she had been making an effort to show herself to be a sophisticated and an impressive young editor from a respected magazine. Then, when she did that, the performance dropped; not only was she underpaid, the gesture said, but she really liked toast. She liked toast even more than she liked being admired.

~

The night before, I had gone out with some friends, and the topic of having children had come up. Everyone had so much to say. One of the men, a sort of Marxist intellectual who was committed to not having children, pointed out that Walter Benjamin had rightly expressed that revolutionary anger and the spirit of sacrifice *is better nourished by the image of enslaved ancestors rather than that of liberated grandchildren.*

The conversation went on for another half hour, before this man's girlfriend, who had not said much of anything until then, remarked, *Being a woman, you can't just say you don't want a child. You have to have some big plan or idea of what you're going to do instead. And it better be something great. And you had better be able to tell it convincingly—before it even happens—what the arc of your life will be.*

HOME

I got out of the cab with my suitcase and felt a sense of peace and calm, standing in front of our home—a pretty apartment on the second floor of a very old house, with its tangled lawn.

I had a memory from our first year together: Miles was standing at the living room window, watching the first snowfall of the year, and turning to me while I was lying on the couch, under a blanket and reading, he held up four fingers. *Four seasons*, he said, because I had once told him that my religious cousin said we should be together four seasons before we decide whether to marry. He said, *We have been together four seasons now.*

I can hear the vacuum cleaner in the next room. Miles spent the last few minutes fixing it. We bought it last week and already I broke it. Now it seems to be working again.

I just went into the living room and told Miles that at my reading in New York, I met a woman who I liked and trusted right away. She told me, as we stood by the bar in the darkened club—she was a little bit witchy, and a little bit psychic—that she could see it: I would have *one vaginal baby* and I would have it for karmic reasons, not because I wanted to.

Miles replied, *If I met some guy in a bar and he told me that one day I'd own a Corvette, I don't think I'd go around telling everyone.*

I had bad dreams again last night. I have had terrifying dreams since my childhood, and I don't know why. Do these dreams visit me to balance out something in my conscious attitude?

no

Am I just cursed by a demon, sort of randomly?

yes

Should I pay any attention to my dreams—imagine they say something real about my life?

no

All they can tell me about is the demon?

yes

Would it be useful to pay attention to my dreams, to learn more about the demon?

yes

So I can fight it?

yes

Is there any chance of me being successful in the fight?

no

Do I fight this demon, which brings me nightmares every night, in a logical and systematic way?

yes

Do I fight it also in random and magical ways?

yes

Should I begin to personify this demon that brings me bad dreams?

yes

Should I visualize a monster?

no

Should I visualize a human being?

no

Should I visualize a spirit or energy?

no

Should I visualize an inanimate object?

yes

A toaster?

no

A knife or hairdryer?

yes

Both?

no

A knife?

yes

I'm thinking of one—it has a black, hard, plastic handle. But it would be more fun to visualize a knife with a wooden handle. Should I switch?

no

Okay, so like the knife in my kitchen drawer. That is the demon that brings me bad dreams, and has, my whole life long. Should I bring it to my desk?

no

Should I take a photograph of it in the drawer?

no

Is it a knife because the demon wants to cut away what is hopeful and optimistic in me?

yes

Does it want to cut away my trust in the world?

yes

Does it have a good reason for doing this?

yes

Because it's a servant of the devil?

no

Is it an angel, rather?

yes

Is it a situation like 'Jacob Wrestling the Angel'?

yes.

JACOB WRESTLING THE ANGEL

That night, Jacob got up and found his two wives, his two maidservants, and his eleven sons, and carried them across a river. After they were across, he sent his possessions over, too. Then Jacob was left alone, and a creature wrestled with him till daybreak. When the creature saw that he could not overpower Jacob, he touched the socket of Jacob's hip, so that his hip was wrenched. Then the creature said, *Let me go, for it is daybreak.* Jacob replied, *I will not let you go until you bless me.* The creature asked him, *What is your name?* Jacob replied, *Jacob.* The creature said, *Your name will no longer be Jacob, but Israel, because you have wrestled with God and man, and you have overcome.* Jacob said, *Please*

58

tell me your name, but the creature said, *Why do you ask my name?* and blessed him there. Then Jacob called the place Peniel, saying, *It is because here is where I saw God face-to-face, and yet my life was spared.* The sun rose behind him as he left that place, limping because of his hip.

So the point is not to strengthen oneself from the struggle, or to win, but to overcome?

yes

In the dream I had last night, Miles admitted that he was not sexually attracted to me. He said, *You have a Robarts sort of energy, which is attractive, but you don't have the sort of body a man would want to do anything with.* I was so hurt by this—Robarts is a library!—and I realized I had to break up with him if he felt that way about my body; how could our sex life ever be any good? I told him he had to move his possessions out by the seventh. He protested and I gave him until the end of the month. Then I felt sad and lonely. When I woke up, Miles was in a good mood. I did not tell him my dream, because in the past, when I've dreamed about us breaking up, it hurt his feelings to hear it. I'm glad I did not tell him this dream, if it has no information about the real world, but only about the demon-angel, which must be overcome. In our dreams, does one see the face of the demon, its always-changing face?

no

Is it the face of the demon, its face which never changes?

yes

The static face of the demon, on which we confer meaning, images and story.

Leloir

Gauguin

I'd like to know more about this demon—which I should personify as a knife, since it wants to cut away what is hopeful and

optimistic in me, and wants to cut away my trust in the world, yet it is an angel. Have these creatures visited humans always?

no

Have they visited us since at least the biblical age?

no

Do we not know much about the frequency or scope of their visits?

yes

Is the way I will overcome the demon-angel the same method Jacob used?

yes

First he wrestles till daybreak. Then the creature touches the socket of Jacob's hip, and it is wrenched. Then the demon-angel asks to be let go, but Jacob refuses. Jacob says he will not let it go until the creature blesses him, so the creature does. Then Jacob names the place where he is standing, a single word that indicates: *Here is where I saw God face-to-face, and yet my life was spared.* Then he limps away with the sun rising at his back. All the fighting takes place at night. That is the first thing I notice. Curiosity or politeness towards the demon-angel comes next. Then the angel gives Jacob a new name. The most important thing is that Jacob continues to fight, even after he is injured, and instead of fear or anger towards the demon-angel, he asks to be blessed. I think that is the most moving part. That opens up something inside me. I wonder what this tells me about the creature. Does the demon-angel want to be loved?

no

Respected?

yes

Can it bless us in ways nothing else can?

yes

Does it want to cut away our optimism, hope and faith, to make us work harder for the optimism, hope and faith we'll need to replace it—the optimism, hope and faith that was taken away in the night?

no

Does it want us to accept God into our hearts, into the empty space where our optimism, faith and hope once lay, before the demon-angel cut it away?

no

Is it presumptuous of me to ask these questions?

no

Does it want to cut away our optimism, hope and faith so that we might humble ourselves, and humbling ourselves, ask to be blessed?

yes

Shall I ask for its blessing when I wake?

yes

Shall I ask for it in my dreaming?

yes

Should I visualize the knife when I'm asking for its blessings?

yes

Should I actually put the knife in my bedroom?

yes

When Miles asks about why there's a knife in the bedroom, should I explain it to him very lightly, very generally, not really getting into it?

yes

Either of these could work. Should it be the knife on the right?
yes

Is this placement okay? I can see it from my bed this way, pretty easily, when I wake.
no

Should I put it here, then?

yes

Is this better still?

yes

Do you want me to go take a picture of it by the window, to see if that's even better?

yes

Well?

no

So over by the mirror?

yes.

~

The first present Miles gave me was a little knife on a chain. I remember so well the way he came into the kitchen, holding it in his hand, not in a box or anything, the chain hanging off his hand and his slightly bent posture, and how loose his jaw was at that moment. Did you dislike the first position, above the door, because that's where one might put a cross—was it too religious?

no

Is it because I look in the mirror often, so I should put it there, reminding me, when I look, of my humility and my needing to be blessed?

yes

It's nice to think that these nightmares are the face of the demon-angel, which must be overcome—but wait! What does *overcome* even mean? Does it mean that at a certain point it will just be so in me—this sense of my own humility, and my needing to be blessed—that the nightmares won't need to visit me anymore?

no

I just read a commentary that suggests Jacob was wrestling with himself—with his new self, now that he is a successful man. As he limps away from the struggle, *the physical and the spiritual are no longer at odds. Together, they accompany him every step of the way as he moves towards his destiny, albeit at a slower pace physically, but spiritually invigorated.* Is what needs to be overcome the opposition between the spiritual and the physical?

yes

Is this related to our humility?

yes

Is Miles's knife a symbol of our humility; the dependence of our love on the fates?

no

The dependence of our love on each other?

no

66

Our dependence on each other, flat out?

yes

Is that why we must be loving?

no

Can I change the topic?

no

Miles said early on that we must always put the other one first, and that if we both do this, everything will be fine. Then maybe it's not such a risk to be dependent on him, because here he is—a strong, intelligent and loyal man—and I have put my dependence on him. But he is going to use his intelligence and love towards putting me first, and the same goes the other way. The risk of loving has never been so clear to me, and how awful it is without trust or faith, which I always find so hard. Will I be able to love him more easily if I accept that I'm dependent on him?

yes

I have never wanted to feel like I'm dependent on a man. I've done everything I could do to avoid it. Yet men are dependent on women, too, and all humans are dependent on things beyond the human. A large tree branch fell down in front of me the other day, as I was walking up the street, and I took it as a sign of good luck, for it could have come down right on my head. Is depending on bigger things part of reconciling the spiritual with the physical?

yes

Is the micro—someone else—easier to look at than *bigger things*, so we can use it as a model to teach us about the nature of our dependence on these bigger things?

yes

I would love to learn trust and faith in love, and to have this lead me towards having trust and faith in whatever the universe brings, and to recognize my dependence on Miles, and his dependence on me, and our mutual dependence on whatever we are all part of, which is so much bigger than us. These nightmares, which have brought an undercurrent of terror to my life—that I might, through wrestling with them, overcome my lack of trust and faith—which means reconciling the spiritual with the physical, which has to do with learning humility and asking to be blessed, just as my thoughts are humbled by the random throw of the coins, and my understanding is dependent on their verdict. Although in the end I will walk away hobbled—older and more physically feeble—I will hopefully emerge more spiritually strong.

~

I woke up this morning with such an abundant feeling of love in me. I felt so much love for the world and was just pulsing with love when I woke. I can't remember ever feeling so great. I *laughed* in my dreams! They were simple—no nightmares. At one point I was in a car with Miles's father and we were laughing happily together. Now there is the sound of church bells in the distance, which I haven't heard from the apartment before.

Coming out of the shower, Miles noticed the knife on the bedroom dresser. *What is this for?* he asked. I answered him sort of vaguely, *Ah, it's just for something I'm writing.* He got a look, like he wanted to know more, but respected my right not to be asked. He said, *Does it have to be that knife?*

I said, *yes.*

My father's mother drew closed the white curtains in her dining room window on Friday nights, even though she lived in a nice brick house in a middle-class neighborhood in Toronto. She did not want people to see her lighting the Sabbath candles and know she was a Jew. Her parents and brother had died in a concentration camp, while she spent the war hiding in Budapest, moving from one person's apartment to another, every few days, before neighbours grew suspicious and started asking questions about her. *The Germans took their lives and the Communists took their property,* my father once told me, about his mother's family. *There was nothing left. Well . . . we were left.*

~

When my mother's mother, Magda, was twelve years old, both her parents died of influenza. They were in their early thirties, and poor—what little money they had was hardly enough to feed their four children. They had no money to visit a doctor, and so died without being seen.

The four orphans were taken in by their mother's cousin, who lived in the same small village as they did. Every morning before school, Magda had to stuff corn into the mouths of the geese, to fatten them for market. She hated doing this. She was constantly hungry through her childhood. She and her brothers would steal and eat the food left over from what was fed to the pigs in the backyard. Instead of going to high school, she went to work as a seamstress.

When Magda was twenty-one, she was deported to Auschwitz with her brothers. There, an older woman she had known from before the war was in the same barracks. This woman was sick, and Magda tried to make it easier for her to be in Auschwitz. One day, Magda found a large stone in the camp, and thought it might be nice for this older woman to use it as a pillow, so she took it and gave it to her. Later, however, Magda realized that the stone was perhaps already being used by somebody else as a pillow, and she felt guilty that she might have stolen it from someone.

The older woman died in the camp. After the war, Magda married the woman's son, George, who was kind to her surviving brothers, and they settled in Miskolc.

~

Magda and George were not an intellectual match. She wrote poetry and liked to talk with neighbors about political events and philosophical ideas. His main pleasures were a good meal and playing cards with his friends. They had one girl, who died as a baby. Then my mother was born.

When my mother was in first grade, Magda returned to high school to get her diploma. There were many adults in her class, and she would sometimes tell her husband about this or that classmate who had decided to quit school. My mother, hearing these stories, often informed her mother that she wanted to

quit school, too. Her mother would say, *Okay, you go out to play.*
Then you can quit school tomorrow.

Around this time, Magda was friends with an elderly woman
without much money, and Magda wanted to help her financially.
But this older woman was too proud to take charity, so Magda
would ask her to come over and help with chores around the
apartment. But before the woman came, Magda would do everything to tidy up, leaving only two plates in the sink for the woman
to wash. Her friends were from all classes and corners of society:
artists, grocers, policemen, clerks.

After finishing high school, Magda attended university to
become a lawyer. She was the only woman in her class. She
wanted to defend child criminals, feeling that no child was
intrinsically bad. My mother remembers her mother studying
long into the night. She finished law school, and nearly gradu-
ated, but at the last moment the school did not let her, for
George had done something illegal: he had smuggled sweaters
from Hungary into Czechoslovakia to sell at a dry goods fair.
Magda was furious. After that, she helped her husband with
the business forever, but she was unhappy with her fate. Now
she would never be a lawyer. She would sell sweaters the rest
of her life.

She insisted my mother become a professional; wanted her
to get a good education, make something of her life, since
Magda could not. So my mother dedicated herself to studying
from the time she was a girl.

All through my mother's childhood and youth, she would
wake up in the house all alone, her parents having risen before
dawn to go sell clothes at a fair. My mother always woke in a

dark, empty home. *No one even opened the blinds.* She would eat her breakfast alone and go to school, then come home again to an empty house. In the evening, her parents would return exhausted from the market, then go straight to bed.

In school, the children sat in pairs, two desks pressed up one against the other, but my mother insisted on sitting alone. Sometimes when another child was home sick, if my mother liked that child's seat-mate, she would go and temporarily sit with them. When Magda found out that her daughter was sitting alone, she told her to stop doing that. She went to the teacher and asked her to make my mother sit with another child. But the teacher defended my mother, saying, *No, let her.*

~

My father left Budapest and came to Canada with his family when he was eleven years old. In his twenties, he met my mother, who was visiting family in Toronto. They were set up by a mutual friend. My father fell in love with my mother, and once she returned home, he sent her many love letters across the ocean. He was an appropriate suitor: a Hungarian Jew, a professional engineer, living in Canada.

On his first visit to Magda's house, Magda observed my father playing on the carpet with a cat, and she warned my studious mother: *He will always be playing.* Magda loved my father and wanted him to marry my mother. My mother wanted to marry him, too.

At my parents' wedding, Magda was suffering from cancer, and after the wedding, my mother felt reluctant to leave

Hungary, fearing her mother's illness might get worse. Her mother, however, pretended she was fine and encouraged my mother to leave. So my mother came to Canada with my dad.

My mother hardly spoke any English. She had to learn a new language and repeat her medical training in this new country. A few months after they moved, my mother's mother died. It was just before Christmas. Along with the terrible grief, my mother felt so guilty, as though by abandoning her mother, she was the murderer. Around this time, her nightmares about her mother began.

On Christmas Day, two years later, when she was twenty-six, her first child, I, was born. All through my babyhood and childhood and youth, my mother slept in the room next to mine, dreaming nightly about her mother.

~

When my mother was a medical resident, she hated treating old ladies who came in to complain about their backaches, when her own mother had died of uterine cancer at the age of fifty-three. She could find no sympathy for these complaining old làdies, when her own mother never had the chance to get old. So my mother became a pathologist instead.

She worked in a hospital in Toronto, doing autopsies and diagnosing specimens under a microscope to determine whether cells were malignant or benign. When she was doing her residency, my father and I would sometimes visit her on weekends, getting lunch with her in the cafeteria during one of her breaks. She once told me that she wanted to be a pathologist because of how beautiful cells look under a microscope—swirling patterns of purple and pink.

When I was little, I would often find my mother sitting in bed under the covers, with pens and markers all around her, highlighting through the heaviest medical textbooks. When I was five years old, my father and I went to visit her in the apartment where she was living for several months, so she could focus on studying for her exams. There seemed to be nothing so glamorous or romantic in the world as a mother who lived alone in an apartment with her colored pens and books. I wanted to grow up to be like her. I wanted to live in an apartment, too, with no one around to bother me. I loved to visit her there.

My mother put all of herself into her work and let our father raise my brother and me. It was wonderful to have such a loving father, and strange to have a mother who was hardly there. I resented how the world spoke of mothers; what they assumed of mothers and what they assumed of fathers. My father was like the other kids' mothers. He came with us on class trips. He knew the names of all my friends and every one of my teachers. He took me to birthday parties and the ballet. He arrived home from work hours before my mother did, and never worked on weekends. I remember racing down the hall when he would come in through the front door after work, setting his briefcase down, and I—wild and dizzy with love—would run into his arms.

A friend once asked me if my mother was dead.

~

My mother wanted a dutiful girl—which I was not—who would obey her and show her respect. She was strict and wanted me to be a doctor, like her, when all I had ever cared for was art. She didn't see what there was to care for in art. The things I loved most had no value for her, so—what felt like an open question to me—of what value to her could I be? Do I remember longing for something I did not have, like the loving gazes and touches of the mothers of my friends? I had a father, who lavished me with love.

Although my parents were eventually unhappy in their marriage—she valued achievement and work; he valued wonder and play—she was happy to have married a man who was a devoted parent, at a time when most men were not. She was relieved she could rely on him to take care of us—to do far more than most men would. In this way, she made the right match. She married the right man for her work, although he wasn't the right man for her happiness.

Today they are sort of like brother and sister—for family is scarce in our family.

When my mother first saw a dead body, she was in medical school in Hungary. It was lying open on a table before her, and glancing over it, she felt a kind of vertigo. She hadn't expected there would be anything more there than blood and bones and viscera, yet some part of her kept looking. Even though she had been raised without God, she was troubled to find nothing else there—no soul.

That is how I felt when I got married, quite young. I had expected that in the moment of marrying something would appear or be born of the moment—something magical, a bubble encasing us, the shiny bubble of Marriage. But just as that autopsied body revealed a startling lack of something to my mother, so in the moment of marrying I felt I'd been tricked: marriage was nothing more than a simple human act that I would never be up to fulfilling.

So I fear will be the first moments in the delivery room, after having my baby laid on my chest, when it will hit me in a similar way as to how those moments dawned: there's nothing magical here either, just plain old life as I know it and fear it to be.

When Miles came over and stood behind me as I was writing, and put his hands on my breasts, I got tense. I got tense because I had just been looking at a picture of a big-breasted girl, and it seemed to me like there was not much for him to touch. I thought he must be thinking about the inadequacy of my breasts. Then he removed his hands. Could he tell that I got tense?

yes

Did he understand that I was feeling insecure about my breasts?

yes

Was he, in fact, disappointed by the inadequacy of my breasts, as he touched them?

no

Oh well. That's too bad. It's too bad I projected that onto him, just as I'm projecting onto you, coins, the wisdom of the universe. But it's useful, this, as a way of interrupting my habits of thought with a *yes* or a *no*. I feel like my brain is becoming more flexible as I use these coins. When I get an answer I didn't expect, I have to push myself to find another answer—hopefully a better one. It's an interruption of my complacency—or at least that's what it feels like, to have to dig a little deeper, to be thrown off. My thoughts don't just end where they normally would. At the same time, by this age, I feel like I have accepted myself on a certain level, so throwing coins is not self-annihilating, which it would be if I still despised myself. Or *do* I still despise myself?

no

Did I ever?

no

No, no, it was all make-believe, even then. Even when it seemed like I did, I was still so grateful to have been born. Is it possible to despise oneself but love the world?

yes

But isn't the self part of the world?

yes

Then I don't understand how it's possible to despise yourself but love the world. I guess a person has to fundamentally feel like they are not part of the world. Is that it?

yes

Is that the essence of despair?

yes

What's the opposite of despair? Joy?

yes

Peace?

no

Happiness?

yes

So the essence of happiness and joy is the feeling that one belongs to the world?

yes

And is of, and part of the world—actually undivided from it?

no

Is *at home* in the world?

yes

At both the microcosmic and the macrocosmic level?

no

Only at the microcosmic level, like in a city, a relationship, a family, or among friends?

no

Only at the macrocosmic level, like in nature, humanity and time?

yes

I made a resolution this year that I would be happy. I so wanted to be happy, sort of at the expense of everything else, but I did not know what happiness consisted of. Now that I know, I will focus on that. Happiness and joy are feeling like you belong to the world, and are at home in the world, at the level of nature, humanity and time.

~

Over the weekend, my father and I watched some home movies that were shot in Florida when I was around nine or ten. In one of them, my mother and brother are in the hallway of a building where my mother's religious cousins owned two condos; we were staying there for a week. My dad holds the video camera, and we are walking down the hall from one condo, the one we were staying in, to the other one, which had a TV. I am performing for the camera, telling my dad to shoot the ceiling fan, and announcing in a slow and deliberately performative voice, *Look at the fan! It goes round and round* . . . like someone selling a house to an idiot.

In the video, my mother leans against the door frame of the second condo, and asks my father if he has the keys, wanting to get inside and away from us. There's a look of disgust on her face as she watches me. *Stop acting!* she says. *Try to live your life.* My parents never agreed on anything, and so my father defends me, *No, she's trying to act, because it's a travelogue, we're moving from our apartment to the other apartment.* My mother addresses him sourly under her breath, *No! I tell her sometimes, 'Be yourself.' But I don't know what 'herself' is anymore. Her acting and 'herself' is completely mixed up.*

For years, that video caused me so much pain, seeing my mother's contempt. When I was younger, watching it, it was all the proof I needed that she did not love me. But now I think her criticisms were correct. Myself and my acting *were* completely mixed up. I wish my mother had helped me with my problems, and expressed them to me in a constructive way, helping me sort myself out. I never understood what she thought was so wrong about me, so I concluded that my whole entire being was wrong. That is the way I have always felt: helplessly wrong, and so desperate to live as a person beyond criticism, whatever that might mean; to prove that I was better than any of the ways she saw me, to do one thing she might admire.

Yesterday morning, my mother and I were sitting in the auditorium at Roy Thomson Hall for a three-hour ceremony in which the entire family had gathered to watch Miles's call to the bar. Soon he would rent an office and start his own practice. There were hundreds of other people there. We were sitting high in the nosebleed seats, with Miles's family all around us, and strangers in the rows in front of us and behind. I began telling my mother what the fortune teller in New York had said to me in the street—that the reason she and I were sad was because three generations of our family were cursed—me, her, and her mother. She got a curious little smile on her face, and when I pressed her for what that smile meant, she said she did not believe it was true.

~

After the ceremony, I was talking to a friend of the family, Sylvia, at the garden party she had organized for her son and Miles. She said it looked good, what was between Miles and me. That's the way it was with *him*—she pointed at her husband's back. She told the story marvellously, of how they first met. It was not what I expected. Both of them had been married to other people. That was twenty-five years ago. Those first years were hard—*it's still hard a lot*, she said. She's not doing her art. Their three kids have grown.

She called my former relationships *narcissistic* because they were all about what I wanted, *my* happiness. With Miles—where I second-guess myself, take pause, consider my behavior and think about what *he* wants—she said that's what raising a child is like; it pushes you to your limits. Being with a man who makes you feel that way, *it's more relational,* she said, and it makes you into a better person, *because you are not necessarily good the way you are.*

She advised me, *have a baby with him,* as though it's something you do to bring the man closer. Maybe this is a bigger part of why women do it than I know. But I know that when a woman has a child to bring a man closer, often the man just gets further away.

Shopping with my mother, only a few years ago, she shook her head at a pregnant woman who we passed in a mall, who was happily holding hands with her husband. *Enjoy it,* my mother said, under her breath. But she didn't mean enjoy the pregnancy. She meant the woman should enjoy the love she was getting from her husband, for pretty soon the husband would meet his baby, and would love it more than he loved her. She said, *Pretty soon you're going to be replaced.*

~

After I had finished talking to Sylvia, I left the dozen guests who were mingling in the garden and went into the kitchen, and saw Sylvia's eldest daughter leaning against the kitchen counter as her two-year-old played on the floor. I said to her, *I'm so jealous of mothers because whatever else happens, they have this person, this thing.* She said, *That's not right. I used to have things.*

I don't have anything anymore. I don't have my work . . . my daughter is her own person. She doesn't belong to me.

In that moment, I saw it was true: her daughter was something apart from her, not her possession or belonging at all.

~

Sylvia's daughter lived around the corner from us until her child was almost two, and for a while I would go over to help out. I have a perfect memory of changing the little one, and a routine we'd get into. As she lay on her back with a new diaper on, I would pull out pants from under the changing table and hold them up before her eyes. *This one?* I'd ask. *Nah!* she'd say in a little voice. *This one?* I'd ask again. *Nah!* she would grin. And it would go on this way as we laughed at our shared predicament, until finally she agreed to put one on.

One time, upon returning home, I related this to Miles, adding that it was the nicest thing that had happened to me in I-don't-know-how-long, and he shook his head, meaning, *Being a woman is the stupidest, most unfortunate thing to be.*

~

Last night, I dreamed I was playing in the sea with my blonde, long-haired, three-year-old daughter. It was warm and we were dancing in the waves, and I thought if a vacation could always be like this, then having a daughter would be a pure joy.

I woke up terrified at three in the morning, wondering, *What if I've suppressed my desire for children so much that my desire is unrecognizable to me?* I remembered that after Miles and I got together, I was alone, walking along the beach in L.A., so lit up with the idea that I might one day have our child, and how aroused I was to think of Miles with a ring around his finger, as my husband in the world; and how erotic I found it, imagining carrying a child, half his.

Sometimes I'm convinced that a child will add depth to all things—just bring a background of depth and meaning to whatever it is I do. I also think I might have brain cancer. There's something I can feel in my brain, like a finger pressing down.

~

Maybe raising children really *is* a thankless task. Maybe there's no reason to thank someone for putting their energies into a human who did not need to be born. Then should we be trying to work against this impulse—as Miles said—pass through our childbearing years without bearing a child, no matter how much we might desire it; but to selflessly and with all our might do whatever we can to avoid it? To find our value and greatness in some place apart from mothering, as a man must find his worth and greatness in some place apart from domination and violence, and the more women and men who do this, the better off the world will be? Miles said we value warring and dominating men, the same way we revere the mother. The egoism of childbearing is like the egoism of colonizing a country—both carry the wish of imprinting yourself on the world, and making it over with your values, and in your image. How assaulted I feel when I hear that a person has had three children, four, five,

84

more . . . It feels greedy, overbearing and rude—an arrogant spreading of those selves.

Yet perhaps I am not so different from such people—spreading myself over so many pages, with my dream of my pages spreading over the world. My religious cousin, who is the same age as I am, she has six kids. And I have six books. Maybe there is no great difference between us, just the slightest difference in our faith—in what parts of ourselves we feel called to spread.

BOOK TOUR

On my first night abroad, in a small restaurant in Stockholm, my thirty-two-year-old Swedish editor began telling me about how she and her girlfriends (all of whom have husbands and children) have one friend who has been with her partner for the last seven years, and this woman is the only one of their original circle from university who doesn't have a kid. She says that her friend and her friend's husband don't want one, but when this friend is not at dinner, all her friends talk about her, and feel sorry for her, and speculate that it is *he* who does not want a child, and really she does. Her life is the focus of much interest. I said that maybe the friend actually *doesn't* want a baby, but it was hard for my editor to accept the possibility; not, I think, because she couldn't imagine some *other* woman not wanting to have a child, but because this friend has been well-cemented in their circle of girlfriends as the one they can feel sorry for, and feel sort of superior to, and who they believe they have special knowledge of (more knowledge than the friend has of herself). They need someone who they feel their lives are better than. She serves an important role.

I thought it must be awful for the friend to have to be still in contact with her university friends. She must know that on some level they pity her and don't believe her account of her life. I wished she could find some new friends, and suspected that she probably *did* have new friends, and perhaps socialized with her university friends only when she had to, which was why she sometimes wasn't at those dinners where her friends gossiped about her delusions and her lack.

~

A tall, dark-haired American writer who I met at the festival said that with women our age, the first thing one always wants to know about another woman is whether she has children, and if she doesn't, whether she's going to. *It's like a civil war: Which side are you on?*

We were at an ordinary bar in Dublin, late at night, packed with young men who were dancing with gusto, enthusiasm and affection under rotating lights. They huddled together, grabbed each other's asses, bumped together, chest against chest, and hit on us without hope. We gave them the chilly edge. Then she went to the bathroom. *You're not leaving me alone here, are you?* I said. While she was gone, I kept my eyes fixed on the dolled-up ladies on the large TV. As I was watching, I thought about how unfair it was that she and I had to think about having kids—that we had to sit here talking about it, feeling like if we didn't have children, *we would always regret it.* It suddenly seemed like a huge conspiracy to keep women in their thirties—when you finally have some brains and some skills and experience—from doing anything useful with them at all. It is hard to when such a large portion of your mind, at any given time, is preoccupied with the possibility—a question that didn't seem to preoccupy the drunken men at all.

~

In Munich, the producer of a half-hour television arts program—short, with straight blonde hair pulled back, who appeared to be about six months pregnant, and who was holding a large, heavy clipboard—overheard me talking to the host of the show. She said that she was forty-one and pregnant with her second child. Pointing at her belly, she remarked, *This is not the only life I could have had. I could have made a different choice. It's not necessary to be a mother—it's just one thing.*

The interviewer was in his mid-fifties. He said he had always wanted a child, but only with the right woman, who he did not meet until he was forty-five. She was in her late thirties then, with a four-year-old son. They discussed what they should do, and she said the decision was his. He finally chose not to, because by then he felt too old.

He said that between him and his siblings, none of them had kids. His parents had split up after twenty years, and he said he thought that was the problem. *What was?* I asked. *The fact that they broke up the family,* he explained, *means we didn't feel obliged to carry it on.*

~

Last night, my Dutch publisher was telling me about how he has two children with his current wife and one kid with his ex. His eldest daughter is twenty-four; the boys are nine and twelve. He said that after the third child, he told his wife, *Enough!* He felt too old to have any more, so he got a vasectomy. But in the years since, he's had many moments of regret, because once the boys got a little older, he said he wanted it again—the experience of cradling an infant in his arms.

He has a friend who, with her husband of thirteen years, was trying to get pregnant. They tried everything, multiple rounds of IVF. Nothing worked. Then the friend had a one-night stand. From this, she became pregnant. She told her husband, and he said he would accept the child as his own, on one condition: the child would never know that some other man was the biological father. The woman could not agree to this, so the couple split up. *Now it is very difficult for her*, he said, *raising the child alone.*

I went to smoke outside the restaurant, and began to talk to a man who offered me a light. He asked me where I was from, and I told him. Then he began talking to me about a gay friend of his in New York: both men in the couple were lawyers. Now they had two children from the womb of one woman, and the eggs of another (asking me, in a heavy accent, *Is this the correct word—egg?*). The women weren't in the lives of the kids, because the men are lawyers, and they wrote up very strict contracts, he said. It had cost his friends a lot of money, particularly to the woman with the womb. *She was always saying, Oh my back aches, oh I need this, oh I need that.* I felt sorry for the woman, who was being portrayed in this way. I kept saying, *She must be poor*—because who else rents out their womb twice? Who else would find the ordeal worth it, never to see the children again? Although I have heard that some women like being pregnant, and want to help out those who can't have kids.

The only reason he was telling me all this was because he learned I was from Toronto—just like his gay lawyer friend. He made sure to add that the children were very adorable and sweet.

~

I had such a nice time the next day, pacing in the sunlight before my 4:30 lecture, realizing how much writing has given me, and feeling so lucky that this passion was mine—right there, in the center of my life. And you are never lonely while writing, I thought, it's impossible to be—*categorically impossible*—because writing is a relationship. You're in a relationship with some force that is more mysterious than yourself. As for me, I suppose it has been the central relationship of my life.

I began thinking about fashion models—these women who, because of their beauty, get to travel the world, and are paid well, and can meet whoever they want, and attract desirable men. I can get some of the same things, too, and I'm not even beautiful, but I can lay my hand on beauty.

~

I showered again this morning with the little hand-held shower, crouching in the tub. At first I found it frustrating, it seemed impossible to get truly clean, but after only three mornings of washing this way, it already feels sensual.

~

Last night, smoking on the balcony of the hotel, on the final night of the festival, this other writer, Adam, said he thought all my questioning about whether to have children would finally lead me to having a child. When I asked why, he said, *You're going to be too curious not to.* He and his wife had two kids. Because I was stoned, I believed what he said. We had just done a panel together, and I wanted to tell him—but I didn't because someone in uniform yelled up at us and told us we weren't allowed to smoke on the balcony—I wanted to tell him that so far, it was having the reverse effect. I could see that it was being taken care of—motherhood. Other people were doing it, so it didn't have to be done by me.

An old woman who was working at the signing table had come up to me after our panel. She was chubby and appealing, with a nice smile and white hair. I had spoken a bit on stage about my deliberations, and she wanted to tell me that she had a daughter who was thirty-five, and that her daughter had once been like me, not knowing whether she wanted to have children or not. Then her daughter got married, and because her son-in-law wanted kids sixty percent, they had them, and now she loves being a mother. She said her daughter is a wonderful mother. Her eyes lit up when she told me that her daughter had *given her* a grandchild, and often once you jump into something, you're happy to have done it.

Adam had overheard our conversation, and as we entered his hotel room from the balcony, he expressed disgust that this woman would come up and tell me what she thought I should do with my life. Yet he wasn't at all surprised. *It's like with abortion,* he said. *People think they own your body; they think they can tell you what to do with your body. Men want to control women's bodies by forbidding them from abortions, while women try to control other women's bodies by pressuring them to have kids.* It seemed so strange and true, and I realized they were both working towards the same end: children. One side spoke from the point of view of the imagined desire of the fetus to live, while the other spoke from the point of view of the imagined joy and fulfilment of the woman, but they both reached the same end.

~

The young Frenchman who drove me to Charles de Gaulle airport this morning said he thought true art was *invisible.* Yet he was encouraging his friends in his mini art collective to make objects that could be sold, because it's hard to make a living as an artist, he said, *if you don't make things; if all you do is create contexts.*

Sitting in the back seat of his car, I wondered if not having children was more like creating a context, while having a baby was more like making a thing. As with an artist who makes objects to sell, it's easy to reward someone for having a child—the meaning of their life is so apparent in its solidness and worth. The course of their future is so clear. To have a child is like being a city with a mountain in the middle. Everyone sees the mountain. Everyone in the city is proud of the mountain. The city is built around it. A mountain, like a child, displays something real about the value of that town.

In a life in which there is no child, no one knows anything about your life's meaning. They might suspect it doesn't have one—no centre it is built around. Your life's value is invisible, like the contexts of that young driver's friends.

How wonderful to tread an invisible path, where what matters most can hardly be seen.

I bought Miles his favorite cologne at the airport in Amsterdam, but I think it was a mistake. This tour was so expensive. These tours always are. I smell too strongly of perfume now, from standing in the perfume store, and spilling some on my coat. I'm going to go to the washroom now to try and wash it off. I can't stand sitting here in this cloud of fumes, this assault of vanilla and fruit.

I am writing this on a plastic bench, waiting for my delayed flight home.

HOME

There is a part of me that isn't taking any of this writing seriously because there's a man in the next room, sleeping. Something about him being there suspends me above all this writing. Because I'm getting something from him, I don't feel like searching for answers. Did my words protect me before, whereas I have no need of their protection now? Were they how I comforted myself before, while I have less need of their comfort now? Do I no longer need to structure the chaos, for love not only structures it, but gives meaning to everything?

Since returning home, I have been feeling that urge—that longing for a holy completeness in the form of a child. Do some women feel this way all the time, carrying a conviction so deep that nothing and no man can shake it? Is that how it is for these women whose bodies strive towards babies—that in their manoeuvrings with men, they feel they are following the highest bidding; the men not useful in themselves, but mainly as a route to something else?

Sometimes I feel it would be so easy to have Miles's baby—his flesh inside mine, his skin so nicely scented, so clean, so smooth; that brain, that heart, mixed with mine. When I described this to Erica, she said, *You're not describing wanting his child in you. You're describing wanting his cock.*

I saw it was true: when I imagine being pregnant, it's more

like the feeling of something lodged inside me—so big, so deep, and feeling so good. I suppose it wouldn't be like that. Then do I really want a child, or do I just want more of him? A child is not more of him. A child is not your boyfriend. When the child grows up and has sex with other people, they are especially not yours then.

~

Last night, I had a really intense dream telling me that my (future) baby had begun his descent to the earth: I saw that it had been given a soul or had chosen a soul and was still very high up and far away, and that this process had begun seven months ago—I mean that seven months ago it had connected to my heart, as if a baby is born first, far in advance, in the mother's heart. The vision was about to end when I desperately rushed to whatever oracle was making it clear, and asked if it was not too late to choose the path along which having this baby was possible. I was reassured that it was not.

~

I think I *do* want a child with Miles. My heart kind of leaps at the thought in a happy way, and it makes me feel light to think about it. I always want it most strongly as I lie in bed beside him. Then perhaps I should talk to him about it. But what would I say? Part of me feels I'm not a real enough woman to pull it off—the making of a child. Other women can pull it off, but I could not. I don't have the energy for all that talking. I would feel like a virgin who doesn't know how to place her hands, or how to place her words. Maybe it's because I don't really feel the desire. Or maybe just because.

I think I don't want to seem ordinary in Miles's eyes; I would rather not have a child than appear that way. Or maybe I can't say it because I don't want to lose face, not after saying so often that it's what I *don't* want. Do I not want to be seen as having changed my mind, or for him to think I'm ridiculous, which he certainly would if I suddenly brought it up? Maybe I would rather leave him than say it.

~

Whenever we have sex lately, I fantasize about Miles coming in me, as though he wants to make a baby, and I'm turned on by the idea that he wants to—more turned on by that than any other fantasy. I used to want to be sexually dominated by him, but lately I don't. If I had a baby, I'd be dominated by the needs of the baby. I don't fantasize about being dominated by the needs of a baby. Yet I still imagine him coming in me.

Perhaps my body is demanding a child of me, and my rational mind is trying to make sense of it. It seems to be amping up its demands, not only on me, but on all the women I know, who are in some crazy heat, wanting to fuck whichever man. Three women I know have left their partners, each in a sudden way, and each for a new man, who they are now either married to or are trying to get pregnant by, as if some part of their bodies suddenly switched on, and pointed at a more real and compelling future.

Does the lizard brain trick the body into singing its ancient song? Of course, you are more than the parts you recognize as you. Perhaps those other parts were quieter in the past, or did their work without being noticed, while now you can see their elbows, their toes sticking out, pulling on the strings of your life. But those same creatures were always there, pulling on the strings of your life. Will you one day feel about the mothering instinct the same way you now feel about the sex instinct, which also suddenly turned on? Like that other passage, you'll resist it, but in retrospect, it took you. You didn't make a choice to go in that direction. Life—nature—pulled your strings. That is why you have no regrets about those years. And where did it land you? In a more interesting place. It resulted in a more interesting time. Is your body now pulling you towards mother-hood, in the same way?

Discussing all this with Teresa, she said she had to tie herself to her bedposts in her late thirties in order not to go down into the street and grab the first decent-looking fellow she saw, and impregnate herself there. She did everything she could to resist her body's urgings, and now she is glad she did.

~

When I think about what I really want, it is a girlfriend for me and Miles. I want a girlfriend around to balance out the masculine he brings, with something more feminine, so our home is more balanced, and my life is, too; so I don't ask him for things he cannot give—the kind of companionship I can only have with a woman. I want a girlfriend and a boyfriend both. I want a woman for us more than I want a baby. I think it would make everything easier, sweeter, more truthful, and more right.

The one time Miles and I had a threesome with a female friend, I felt, *This is heaven, this is everything I have ever wanted in my life. This satisfies every last part of me.*

I had a dream last night that Miles was kissing another woman on a park bench. He seemed to think there was nothing wrong with the way he was kissing this woman's hair, or how they touched tongues. It was clear how much she wanted him. Angrily, I walked away—as if to throw out some garbage— then I walked back. I told him that if he was going to carry on like this, I didn't want him at all.

I woke up crying. When Miles saw me, he got upset and said I shouldn't be crying on account of my dreams. He said he would be ashamed if his nightmares led him to wake up crying. But the dreams play on real feelings in me!—feelings of being abandoned. Then I get sad and cry, which makes him in fact abandon me.

I am a blight on my own life. How can I stop being a blight on my life? It is not right to be a blight on the bounty of life. It's not right to always be sitting here, crying. Outrun your tears—that's all you can do. Outrun your tears like an athlete every day. Outrun your tears like someone with faith. Okay, I will outrun my tears and win.

~

I smoked some pot to get rid of the tears. It's a week before my period begins. Days ten and six and five and one before my period comes are the worst. The rest of the days aren't so good, either.

When I am high, terror replaces the tears. Is that what the tears are masking? Terror that a month has passed without me getting pregnant? Is that what PMS is—some primal fear, maybe of death, or of not having reproduced? Or anger at Miles for not getting me pregnant, just wanting to push him out of the house and out of my life and find a man who will? I felt happier before I was high, although I wanted to cry. Now I'm paranoid, but not as teary. Which is better? It was better before.

~

What to make of God's two faces, the all-accepting and loving New Testament Ovulating God, and the vindictive and rageful Old Testament PMS God? How to reconcile these two within my own body?

To try and understand my moods: my two weeks of unhappiness—PMS, the luteal phase. Then a few days of bleeding. Then a week of mild newness—the follicular phase—when my body is preparing for new life, and ideas come to me easily. Then a few days of ovulating—those days of sparkling joy, when my body most wants to fuck, and nothing in my life feels off.

Maybe if I can predict this cycle, I won't have to take my moods as personally, or do such elaborate contortions to escape them, but can see them for what they are: part of nature, like clouds are part of the sky. Maybe my moods are evidence of how a human is part of time, or is bound to time, or *is* time. The female body, in particular, expresses time and is close to time. When the blood comes out, another month has passed. Erica said, *Actually, I think 'the soul of time' is a pretty accurate way of describing PMS. It's not just a metaphor. It IS the soul of time. That's why it's so unpleasant.*

PMS

This morning, Miles implied that I was not someone a man could build a life with or rely upon. I don't think I've done anything to signal this, but it's true that whatever you are inside, other people will see. There's no hiding yourself from other people. What's the point in acting sweet and accommodating to others when I'm a stranger to myself? What's the good in pointing morning smiles at Miles, or trying to get smiles from him in the morning, when I feel such a blackness in my chest?

Tears and more tears this morning. Not actually crying, but the feeling of wanting to cry. Confusion, neglect. Miles abruptly leaving the room, my feelings trailing off into nowhere, no safe home for my feelings inside him. He walks away before I've even begun.

~

Are my qualities of deceitfulness—which he pointed out I had, which he said all women have—part of the biological imperative? That in order to breed and raise children, morality has not to matter? The only thing that matters is the life of the child, while all other values are relative? Is that how my brain has developed over millennia? If I choose now—decide it, wasting no more time—*not* to have children, can I set myself on a course of reforming my mind, making myself unable to lie or deceive, as if the world of living people, and just these living bonds, matter most of all—having the same kind of accountability as an accountable man? Just as a man might try to rid himself of all entitlement, violence, and need to dominate, could I eliminate from myself my desire to gossip, my petty interest in other lives—especially the darkest parts of the lives of all my female friends—and instead take responsibility for my actions and words, having decided that I won't ever meet a future with children, and all the joys and gratifications of that? To make myself over—use my brain and be unrelenting—and pull myself out of my cloud, rather than remain in it like someone prepared to mould her morality in such a way that its highest purpose is to secure a good life for her child—with all the lies the body tells the mind, and all the tricks it plays. To make sure my body plays no more tricks, and for nothing to be said by me that isn't true. To become like that, I will have to work harder, endure and cause pain—not masochistically torture myself or dwell on my failures or brood miserably over a future that might not come, but will the future I most want. I'll have to remove my feminine self-doubt, which exists out of politeness; remove my second-guessing, that utter waste of time; work harder; think harder—all the violence I will have to do to my own softness, which has always been such a comfort! I shudder to think of how I have let myself fall into the deepest sleep, like a fairy-tale princess, wasting her life in dreams. And the sleep will continue if I don't wake up, shake myself and not lie to anyone anymore. I will have to become one of the straight ones, one of the unflinching, who suffer the consequences of whatever they say and do.

This fog of sleepiness that is my femininity, which has often threatened to drown me—it has to be guarded against, for it has so much power. It wants me to lose myself in child-rearing, to the exclusion of so much—tempting me with those simple joys and those private little accomplishments.

What if I pursue being a bad woman and don't breed—pursue failing biologically? Where is the realm of privacy? Only in failure. Only in our failures are we absolutely alone. Only in the pursuit of failure can a person really be free.

Losers may be the avant-garde of the modern age.

~

In my dream last night, I was looking at my breasts in a mirror. They were hanging so low on my body—at the level of my belly button. I was crying, depressed about them hanging so low. I cried out, in tears, *My breasts are too low!* Then I looked at them closer, and saw there were five nails in each breast, and that my breasts were actually hoofs, and the reason they hung so low was so that I could use them to walk.

Last night I saw Marissa, her hair and outfit immaculately arranged as if for a camera. We had met years ago when I wrote a profile about her for a magazine. She had just come from a day of shooting a series she had written and was starring in. I hadn't seen her in ages. The last time, she had been married to an actor who at the time was less successful than she was, and who, upon her return from L.A., would move into her condo with her. I remember the feeling I got from her about him—that he was someone to help her in her work. Last night, over dinner, I learned they were getting divorced. Marissa is thirty-eight. She said that many of her girlfriends didn't want to have children, were happy just to live with their partners. She said *she* wanted to have children, but it had never felt right with her husband. Her thoughts were always on a man in Italy—a film director who she says she truly loved. She says she loved him all throughout her marriage. When her marriage was over, she wrote him a letter about what her feelings were, and had been since he kissed her many years ago. But for the director, the email had come too late. He said he'd had—a long time ago—to let go the idea of being with her. Now he was with another woman, and although he did not love this woman, even if he wasn't with her, it would still be too late.

Now Marissa had neither man. Newly single, she couldn't help but feel outside the mainstream of life, as though she had lost a certain status in the world, especially among women. She was *just this floating thing, a potential threat*. She felt bitter about her husband. The problem with him was that *he had not worn the pants in the relationship*, so she didn't totally respect him. *It's not sexy*, she said. She thought he had benefited greatly from their marriage, because he was now a success. But it had been awful to be with another actor—she never would be again. He had taken things she had said over dinner and would say them in interviews as though the ideas were his own. She kept trying to escape him to work on her screenplay—two months here, one month there—and would work well when they were apart. Then he would come and visit her, and she would lose the thread and tell him to go home.

The director in Italy sounded like pure fantasy to me, but the way she saw it, they were constantly being brought together. She never wrote anything inspired by her husband, yet she wrote a whole script inspired by *him*. And wasn't it fate that they were both in London at the same time? Yet, I pointed out, they didn't *get* together in London, nor did they get together in Vancouver or Rome. She insisted that fate kept bringing them together, but the way I saw it was: every time they were brought together, they never actually *got* together, so maybe it was fate's way of saying: *You're not meant to be together—just look! Every time I bring you close, nothing ever happens.*

When we left the restaurant, I walked behind her and noticed her ankle boots—very high heels—and that the heels had been rubbed away at a slight angle, each point pointing inward. To see her wobbling like a witch, I felt deeply moved. She seemed so poor and vulnerable from behind.

When I was out with Marissa, she pointed out that *men like to come in their partners.* Although this should have been obvious, I had never thought about it before, and it remained stuck in my head for weeks. I decided to finally get an IUD.

The insertion was the most painful thing. As the doctor was working it inside, I shouted in my head, *Stop! Stop!* but I let it be put in. Then I found myself hobbling off the table and out of the examination room, even as I tried to tell myself there was no reason for me to hobble.

The entire time it was inside me, I felt like there was a sharp-toothed bear trap within. I could not walk properly, I tried not to move, I could not forget it was there. Everything Miles said made me upset, for I resented that I had this thing inside me—as I thought—*for him.* It made me feel plugged up and sad. And although I didn't want to get pregnant, I found I liked even less the idea that I could not. It felt like my womb was made of cold hard plastic and metal coil, as though the innermost part of me was a torture device, although I did not know what part of me it was torturing. It was as if a sensitive, mushy, thumping animal inside—which I hadn't even known about—had been captured and stilled.

After ten days, I could stand it no longer, and I returned to have it taken out. Leaving the hospital, my love for Miles felt

unleashed. I had to admit, sheepishly, that the slimmest possibility that I might get pregnant made me love him even more. Just
the possibility worked some charm.

~

Last night, out with another writer friend, I told her about
the IUD. She said, *I could never get an IUD—I couldn't do it, it
wouldn't be right for me.* I felt excluded from some deeper
knowledge she had. She was a private person, someone
who seemed to know herself. I said, *I bet you always consult
your heart.* She agreed that she did.

I don't think I have a heart—a heart I can consult. Instead, I
have these coins.

~

Are the fantasies that visit us, of living other lives—like living with
children if we don't have them, or living without if we do—taboos?
yes
Are we supposed to build a conscious relationship with these
taboos, so we might feel more at home in the world, on a
macrocosmic level?
yes
How are we to do that? By challenging these taboos with our
behavior?
no
By challenging them conceptually, in thought alone?
no

Instead of challenging them, should we be trying to bind the taboos with our lives, and so create a synthesis in our living?

yes

Do we do this by choosing, with great determination, the life we're living now, with the conviction that we will never live the taboos that call out to us?

no

Jacob names his wrestling place *Peniel*. Is he naming a personal taboo, in doing this?

yes

I suppose for him the taboo was that man could stand face-to-face with God. That idea must have frightened him as much as to be a mother frightens me. Do we synthesize taboos with our lives by creating spiritual or religious practices around them, giving them a place, but a place that is safe?

no

Do we synthesize taboos by taking on a new name—as Jacob's name became Israel?

no

Do we synthesize them by narrating them, by telling ourselves stories about our wrestling with them?

yes

Is the idea of being a mother a taboo for me, personally?

yes

Then must I synthesize this taboo with my life by telling a story about wrestling with it?

yes

But it takes a long time to tell a story, meaning that when we are done, we walk away hobbled—older—but hopefully more spiritually invigorated. Jacob named his story 'Peniel,' which means, *Here is where I stood face-to-face with God.* What am I standing face-to-face with? The prospect of motherhood?

yes

In the story of Jacob, the angel blesses him there. Yet *wait*—what does it mean to be blessed? That the thing we are wrestling with wishes us well?

no

That our wrestling will take care of us forever?

yes.

~

My brother feels it was an unfair burden placed on him to have been forced to live without having been asked. I feel the opposite—that life is a beautiful and incredibly rare gift whose debt I will forever be in—and that I must spend my days paying back this debt.

Where do I get this idea of my indebtedness from? And who am I paying it back to? And why must it be the only thing in my life—paying it back? Could having children be a way of repaying the debt? For some it must be, but it doesn't feel that way to me. I know how hard it is to have a child, but for me it would feel like an indulgence—an escape. I don't feel I deserve those pleasures. Having a child does not relate to the duties that feel bound to my life.

~

What is wrong with living your life for a mother, instead of a son or daughter? There can be nothing wrong in it. If my desire is to write, and for the writing to defend, and for the defence to really live—not for just one day, but a thousand days, or ten thousand days—that is no less viable a human aspiration than having a child with your mind set on eternity. Art is eternity backwards. Art is written for one's ancestors, even if those ancestors are elected, like our literary mothers and fathers are. We write for them. Children are eternity forwards. My sense of eternity is backwards through time. The farther back in time I can go, the deeper into eternity I feel I can pierce.

I always thought that if I could find the first boy I loved, and love him, I would love him and remain with him for the sake of eternity.

And that is sort of what I did. Although we didn't come together until I was thirty-two years old, Miles was the first boy I longed for after moving out of my parents' house after high school ended. Everything grew quiet the first moment I saw him. He was standing and smoking in front of a repertory cinema, after the movie let out—lanky, with blacker than black hair, browner than brown eyes, and eyeliner. He was taller than anyone else in the crowd, and elegantly dressed, and was looking off with shy, intelligent eyes. Standing a short distance from him outside the theatre, I said to my boyfriend, *There is the most beautiful person I have ever seen.* Fifteen years later, it was still true.

The feeling of tears was in me when I woke, but they weren't in me last night, alone. I like being alone. It is hard to be around other people. Alone, one feels the whole universe, and none of one's personality. Maybe it is the feeling of my personality that brings me to tears. Where there is no personality, there cannot be tears.

This is the also same age as when your mother was miserable, and also constantly in tears. It could be a biological phase. Or it could be the choices you've made.

Last night you said you'd forgive yourself if you made a mistake. If you made a mistake, you said you'd forgive yourself. *I'm sorry—I forgive you—I apologize—I forgive you—I forgive you—I forgive you—I forgive you.* You weren't sure whether you had done something wrong, but you said you'd forgive yourself, although you were unsure.

~

Last night, I dreamed that Miles wanted to have a baby with me—really, really wanted to. There was such a sweet, serious longing in him that I started to think that maybe it would be a good idea to go ahead, just rush ahead with that feeling of excitement—it was like being pulled along—although secretly I felt I didn't want to. So I said *no* to Miles in my dream. I felt that if I said yes, I would abandon my child. Still, there was something flattering or totally awesome in him wanting to have a baby with me. No one had ever asked that of me before.

Waking up, I said to Miles, *It might be nice to have a child.* He said, *I'm sure it's also nice to get a lobotomy.* All the work he's done these years to build himself up into the sort of person he can respect—talking about throwing that out the window; how the hardest thing in life is to really make something of yourself. He said, *Two people who can help hundreds of people—that they should put their energies into one half-person, each? This is a human life we're talking about here! Why do people—as soon as things are good—suddenly want to change everything?*

~

Teresa said that people are dominant in either thinking, or feeling, sensation or intuition, and that psychic health is using all of one's faculties. In order to know my mind about children, I'll have to use feeling more. I remember once reading that all philosophers are ugly: they have too big a nose, or too big a forehead, or ears that are too big, from all that thinking. I never understood it before, but I understand it now: the philosopher unbalances herself. The trick to life is having your nose, forehead, and ears be all the same size. Then are there other places I should be spending time, besides in my thoughts?
yes
In my body?
yes

In my senses?

yes

Should I try to sense more things?

no

Should I try to sense what I do sense, more consciously?

yes

What does that mean? With more discernment?

no

More love?

yes

Is consciousness love?

no

Does consciousness *create* love?

yes

In every case?

yes.

I received two *soul of time*–like messages in the fortune cookies last night.

One said, *Stop searching. Happiness will find you.* The other said, *Your future will be harmonious.* These gave me the same feelings as the words *the soul of time* does—that maybe I don't need to be doing as much as I have been doing, on the level of trying to push my life down one path or another. And maybe there are some areas of life in which one never knows. Or maybe part of me thinks that when it comes to something as profound as a human life existing or not, it would be wrong to take it too strongly in my hands, or decide too vigorously either way.

After all, it's not only my life we're talking about. It's Miles's life, and the life of the child, and everyone that child will ever meet, and not meet, and whoever might come from them, and whatever they might do in the world. Who is it for me to bring all this unfolding into being? Maybe it's no more for me to decide, than it is for Miles to decide, or my father to decide, or my country to decide. I am in the world, and whatever I do affects other lives. Then it should all be pretty loose, my fantasies for my future, for they each involve everyone else. Why should I strenuously make something come true for me, when that fate will manifest in other lives as well?

I don't know why I don't do the obvious thing—instead of fantasizing about other lives, why not try to imagine what it's like to be me, and live the life I'm living now—fantasize into the life that's actually mine? The first time I ever had this thought, it gave me such a deep thrill, almost a sexual thrill, as if I was having sex with myself. The feeling lasted only a second—a brief spark of power that came from inhabiting my actual life. Then why don't I choose to do this all the time, since it is the truth? Maybe it felt like too much power—perhaps the power of binding the physical with the spiritual—if the spiritual is my imagination, and the physical is my actual life.

Then erase the boundary and bring them closer.

~

Is this way of thinking connected to *the soul of time*?
no
Will I ever figure out what it means—*the soul of time*?
yes
Will I be able to express it in this book?
yes
Should I end this section and begin another one, with that aim in mind?
yes.

~

When I was a teenager, my boyfriend and I lived in a rundown house where all the teenagers went. He and Miles were close friends, so Miles was always around. I respected and admired him, in his dignity, quietness, and his intelligence. At parties, he would lean against a wall, alone. He possessed something romantic that enchanted us all—the way he moved, smoked, dressed and talked.

In the decade following, every time we were in the same city, Miles and I would hang out. When we were around twenty-five years old, he was living in Montreal, and I was just visiting. After seeing a movie, we took a long walk through the city together. At the end of our walk, we stopped by his apartment, and as he leaned against the window of a shop, he told me that he had recently learned he was going to be a father.

I was shocked. None of my friends had children yet. Yet I very quickly could see it. Miles had always seemed so in control of himself, but there was something not in control about him, too—something vulnerable, which could allow life to slip right through his hands. I thought, *Of course it would be Miles—to accidentally knock a girl up. How many women has he slept with, anyway? And who could say no to a baby from him?*

How could I know that, years later, the daughter that he was telling me about, would be a bit my daughter, too?

This afternoon, I went to the fertility clinic for the final of a series of three appointments, to check on the possibility of freezing my eggs. Over the past few weeks, they had done all sorts of tests. I sat on the thirteenth floor of an office tower, in an orange waiting room with some couples and women alone. One woman held a golden-haired toddler who played on the floor—and the other women gave her space. She sat alone on a connected embankment of chairs, while the rest of us gathered more in a clump—out of respect for her or resentment.

Finally, I was called in. A woman sat behind a long glass table that was covered in a mess of papers, wearing a white coat that I couldn't interpret: Was she a doctor? A nurse? A lab technician? How seriously was I to take her? She opened my file and said, *Congratulations—it's good news!* She smiled warmly and said my ovaries were young, *like fresh figs.* I burst into tears. How could my body betray me in this way? Didn't it know anything about us—about what I truly desired?

Leaving the clinic, it was nearly dusk. The sky was bruised and purple, like a fresh fig. Then it began to rain.

Walking home under construction scaffolding, I thought, *No. You are not going to freeze your eggs. You should be able to figure out what you want and get it before the time runs out.* The procedure would cost way more than I had, and I worried that the hormones would hurt me, or that it would hurt my relationship with Miles—make me too emotional to bear Miles, or be borne. Indecision has always been with me, but I didn't want it to dominate my life more than it has already done. Getting my eggs frozen would have been like freezing my indecision. I couldn't reveal my weakness to myself in such a tangible way.

Maybe I feel betrayed by the woman inside of me who can't bring herself to do this thing. Or maybe I feel betrayed by my mother, for not devoting herself to me and creating whatever loving memories must be created in a child to make her want to repeat the process again. Or maybe it's a part of me that goes deeper than that—my lifelong desire to leave my family and never be part of a new one. I did not grow up imagining that after leaving my family of origin, I would go off and make my own. I figured you grew up and out of your own family, more and more each year; that you increasingly tried to win your independence—your freedom and solitude in this world.

All my life, whenever I pictured having children, I never considered the pleasures and joys it would bring. All I could ever see was the suffering—the terrible pain of having a child, and worrying about it, and loving it.

I remember how last summer on the beach, Miles's daughter and I walked together along the shore. I had determined that I would discuss with her why her father and I probably weren't going to have a child together, since earlier on the trip she had asked me about it, and I didn't know what to say. As we walked along the sand with our towels wrapped about us, I said that even that when I was her age, I had never dreamed of being a mother. Even as a young girl, it was something I had not wanted to do. I wanted to have boyfriends, and make art, and have interesting conversations and friends. Then the most honest words pushed themselves from my lips: *I wanted to be free.* She thought about this for a moment, and then said, *That sounds pretty good, too.*

~

Last night, I dreamed that Miles and I had a little boy. He was three or four years old. Very sweet and nice, ordinary little boy. I was carrying him around like a child carries a cat, against the front of my body, legs dangling. Then I put him down and looked at him, and he looked a little like Miles, with Miles's eyes. It was a very calm and ordinary thing.

~

Should I have a child with Miles?

no

Should I have a child at all?

yes

So then I should leave Miles?

no

Should I have an affair with another man while I'm with Miles, and raise the child as Miles's own, deceiving him about the provenance of that child?

yes

I don't think that's a good idea. Are you saying I shouldn't have a child with Miles because it would be too stressful on the relationship, and on each of us, individually?

yes

Then should I have Miles's child but raise it with another man?

yes

Should I get pregnant this year?

no

Next year?

yes

How old will the child be when we separate? One?

no

Two?

yes

And how old will the child be when I find another man? Three?

no

Four?

no

Five?

no

Six?

yes

And will those four years be a big pain in the ass?

no

Will they be kind of a joy?

no

Will they be like any other years?

yes

Will I love the child more than anything?

yes

Will the child be a girl?

no

An attractive child?

no

A plain child?

no

A drop-dead gorgeous child?

yes

Is any of the above true?

no

Is there any use in any of this, if none of it is true?

no

Even if you said yes, it wouldn't matter. You don't mean anything to me. You don't know the future, and you don't know my life, or what city I should be in, or what I should be doing, or if I should have a child with Miles or not. You are complete randomness, without meaning, and you are not showing me the way. That can only be determined by mining my own heart, and looking at the world around me; thinking deeper and more clearly, and not being so insecure that I should need you to tell me what's what. And yet, you have shown me some good things.

yes

But that is just me picking up the good in all the nothing you have shown me. Life involves making a decision so the spirits can rush in. But a decision takes knowledge and faith, which I lack. And yet: I do like the idea of having a drop-dead gorgeous child with Miles.

Nearing home after finishing some errands, I ran into Nicola, who I hadn't seen since grade school. We recognized each other, and stopped to catch up on the sidewalk. She has four children, and is trying to return to the working world, and she congratulated me on the success of my latest book. I said apologetically, *Well, writing is the only thing I do.* I don't cook or do laundry, exercise or go out much. I just sit in my bed and write. I said that I feel like a weak and pale child compared to everyone else.

I believe I want to have adventures, or to breathe in the day, but that would leave less time for writing. When I was younger, writing felt like more than enough, but now I feel like a drug addict, like I'm missing out on life. Not having a child allows a slip into sludginess, into the decadence of doing nothing but sitting before a computer, typing out words. I feel like a draft dodger from the army in which so many of my friends are serving—just lolling about in the country they are making, cowering at home, a coward.

When Nicola learned I was thinking about having a child, she said, *You should go and spend some time with people who do have children, watch them and see what it's like.* I thought, *I don't even want to spend one second doing that.*

~

In my dream last night, I looked down and my breasts seemed to be the soggy breasts of an old woman. Then I realized they were not soggy breasts, but two flaccid penises. When I emailed Teresa about the dream, she replied, *Breasts are what give life, while phalluses represent a creative or generative power—generating works of culture or art.*

Looking away from the computer, I remembered my first weekend with Miles, in the room he was renting in the small town where he was attending law school. We were on the floor by the fireplace, and we didn't yet know that we were together. I was talking about disappointing ex-boyfriends, and he said, *If you ever need someone to be strong for you . . .* and I saw his body solidly there, offering itself to me.

~

The next day, I went over to Nicola's house and her baby was there. A Christmas tree stood in the corner of the living room, hung with ornaments and tinsel, pine needles all around. She asked me to go and sit with the baby—who she plopped on my stomach as I lay down on the carpet. Then she went into the kitchen and finished washing up dishes. I watched the baby as best I could, but I felt edgy—I didn't want to be there. There were other things I wanted to do. I played with her toys before her ten-month-old eyes. Then I thought I should hold her, and I held her facing away from me, so she could see the world.

When Nicola was done with the dishes, she returned to me and her baby, and held the baby facing her body, and the baby seemed happy, turned into that warmth. I was relieved that Nicola had come, so that we could leave soon and talk. Realizing how much I wanted to get away, I felt bad towards her child, and guilty.

What had I been so anxious to go and do? What is a woman—who is not a mother—doing that is more important than mothering? Is it possible to even say such a thing—that there is anything more important for a woman to do than mother? I know a woman who refuses to mother, refuses to do the most important thing, and therefore becomes the least important woman. Yet the mothers aren't important, either. None of us are important.

~

Over the next few weeks, I started feeling bad around Nicola, both better than her and ashamed. Why do I think it could matter to Nicola if I don't have kids? Living one way is not a criticism of every other way of living. Is *that* the threat of the woman without kids? Yet the woman without kids is not saying that *no* woman should have kids, or that you—woman with a stroller—have made the wrong choice. Her decision about her life is no statement about yours. One person's life is not a political or general statement about how all lives should be. Other lives should be able to exist alongside our own without any threat or judgment at all.

~

How stupid! How could I have been so wrong about myself for so long—imagined I could have what Nicola has; a marriage, a house and children. The mistake was taking myself as someone for whom all the riches in the world were waiting, when only one is—writing this now. Whatever I have achieved is a grand prize, and more than I had a right to expect. When did I start thinking of writing as the path to a bourgeois life? That it could get me there and keep me there? When did I become so greedy? When did I start thinking that all the riches should be mine? To be a thirty-eight-year-old woman and want to be respectable in all the ways Nicola is. I went shopping with her on Dundas Street, and we bought some small, pretty things. She encouraged me to buy even more—a glass flask, a white candle. For about a month, our friendship made me feel normal, as if I was like her— on her path, fantasizing about a family. But standing inside her house as her three boys raced around, I realized that my fantasies were misplaced—they wormed inside me like a disease. I mis- took someone else's life for what could be my own. But you cannot take a misunderstanding, and try to build a life on it. You cannot build a life on the misperception that you are someone who could have it all—if only you kept to the path. Even if you could have *some* of those comforts, for some of the time—con- vince someone to marry you, or have a child with you—it would be a mistake, a life built on a misunderstanding of who you are inside. You are not someone who could steer the ship of a house and a marriage and children, the way that Nicola can. Look at her life like a beautiful ocean liner, a grand old steam liner passing by—see that life as it waves at you from the deck. Those promises and pleasures were never meant to be yours. You had a great time imagining they could be, working yourself up into a real lather: *Should I? Should I? Should I choose it? Should I?* But the real ques- tion is, *Could* you? No, you could not. It was just a fantasy, and the most common one in the world. Women will always tell you of how they have done it so easily. But you know what you should be grateful for: following this tiniest thread of freedom, which is to write. That is all you ever truly wanted, so don't vainly throw it away. Don't throw it away chasing even more riches—more than what you're owed. You are owed nothing, and what you do have—this expanse of freedom—do not gamble it away. A life of a house and marriage and children is no better than what you have now. Or perhaps it *is* better—far, far better. But your place is not there. It is here. Don't go looking for more than your share; do not want what *a woman* wants. You are not a woman who wears a diamond ring—the sort of woman, like Nicola, who gets what she wants from a man. For a month you thought you could be. That is why you were so anxious. *Could it be me?* you asked yourself. *Could it? Could it?* No. If you had a child, you'd leave it. If you had a marriage, you'd leave it. You left your marriage. You left your house. Those things were not for you. Nicola said, *You guys should have kids!* But she was fooled by your young-enough body, your sweetness and your smiles. The world is less perceptive than you give it credit for. The world is fairly stupid, and it's stupid about you, too. Be grateful for Miles, and this apartment right here, and being able to write, which is the one thing you asked for, and should continue to be. Just because you get one thing, doesn't mean you get it all. One thing is not the beginning of all.

~

That night, I dreamed I was walking across a small stage before a large audience, in a makeshift graduation gown, to receive a diploma and flowers. As I walked back across the stage with tears in my eyes, my feelings started to overwhelm me. I made myself really *look* at the audience—*look* into their faces. Mostly I knew no one, and I realized that no one was paying attention to me. I thought in my head that it was silly to get so emotional about *a rite of passage of the middle class.*

BLEEDING

I was giving a reading in a church, in a village on a lake. Walking through one of its pretty neighbourhoods, I passed a little house that had, on its front lawn, a handmade wooden sign with shooting stars, a moon, and the palm of a hand. When I knocked, a middle-aged woman came to the door. She was wearing a pink sweater, and her hair was short and fair. She led me to a card table she had set up by the front window. I sat in a wooden chair across from her, and she draped a dark blue velvet fabric over the table.

I've never done a reading on this cloth before, but I don't like a slippery surface when I do a reading, and this helps.

She dealt the cards. *Okay, what's going on in your life? What's good and what's not good? What's working and not working? Once you figure that one out, it's a huge tool.*

Before I could answer, she got up and went to the couch and retrieved her blue-framed glasses. Putting them on as she returned, she said, *Sorry, these new cards are very dramatic. I need to wear my glasses to see them.*

When she returned, I answered her question: *I feel sort of sad and stressed out, kind of confused and depressed a little bit, like I can't get started or something. And I feel like there's a new phase of life I cannot reach—I feel sort of stuck in the old one. And my brain feels a little bit stuck. And then I'm finding that emotionally things are hard for me with my boyfriend, and I'm never quite sure how much of the problem is him and how much of it is just me.*

She said, *Oh, that's a good one. Once you figure that one out, it's a huge tool.*

~

Protective shield! Sorry!—I feel no protective shield with you. Very often I sit down with people and I'll feel nothing, and I'll say to the person, *Your protective shield—do you think it's made out of brick or curtain? Is it Plexiglas? Could you close your eyes and visualize taking it down, please?* Once they do that, I can do the reading, because I can't read through the protective shield. But you don't have one, which either means you're psychic yourself, or you don't have a boundary.

Now, this first card is the Three of Wands. You've walked to the end of something, and you think there's nowhere to go. But I think this end is self-imposed. Perhaps this card is saying you've walked to the end of the real world—the concrete. See? The woman's standing on concrete? And if you look—you see how there's a point at the end?—like a sewing machine point, almost? It leads down to a spot in the river. There's something in you that knows how to keep walking, but something's stopping you. And what's stopping you is . . . grief. I don't know what the grief is. But it has nothing to do with your boyfriend. It's there from before you ever met him, and it's a quiet grief. You don't feel it every day, but it's there all the time. It may be that you're porous and the grief isn't yours. Does your mother have a grief?

Yes.

Well, it might be that you were born with your mother's grief, like it got implanted in you as an energy ball. I feel a really strong energy from you, and it's like, whatever that energy is, you're a baby growing inside your mother's body, and your mother has this ball of grief or sorrow or negativity, and then it goes into your body, and you're born, and you're walking around with your mother's grief and sorrow, and you don't even know it! But it's gnawing at you.

There's a way of saying, *Could you please send that ball of pain back where it belongs, if it isn't mine?* Like actually say, *I'm sending this back now. And please send it back in the most healed and loving form it can go. But I don't want it, it's not welcome, and it's not helping me.* So there we have it. I think that's what's causing your road to end . . .

The next card is the Ten of Swords—the most painful card in the deck. There's something . . . chunks of you . . . are falling down. But look! Strangely, the bleeding is going up, not down. It's not coming out of your vagina or going down your legs. It's going up! Why is the bleeding going up? Softening your brain? This is a hard one . . . I have to feel the card.

~

As she felt the card, her eyes closed. I thought, *Maybe blood that goes down is period blood. It softens the lining of the uterus. And bleeding that goes up is thinking blood. It softens the lining of the brain.* When I was thirteen, the year before I first got my period, I often woke in the middle of the night and felt a tickle of blood at the back of my throat, just as it was beginning to drip down. I would rush to the toilet, head tilted back, and push a wad of toilet paper to my nose as it grew wet and red, replacing it, and replacing it, sitting on the toilet through the long night, endless hours of thinking nothing at all.

~

Okay, I've got something in my mouth. Has it got to do with your voice? Were you able to ask for what you needed from your mother, as a little girl?

I don't think so.

What about what you ate as a girl?

Cheddar cheese and chicken soup?

Pardon me. I'm not understanding. Maybe I need to look in the crystal ball now. Okay, hold on. Turning on the ball . . . I'm slow at this because it's new, so it might take a minute . . . Okay, now I see it! Something's dangling, and it is making me feel a little bit sick. You're sitting in front of a computer . . . what does that have to do with it?

That's what I do all the time.

Pornography?

No. I think it's just writing.

Is there something about your back being to the room when your boyfriend's there, and you're sitting at the computer?

Well, we did argue the other day, and I was at the computer and he was standing behind me.

Okay. I know this sounds very weird and silly, but it's coming into my mind, and I find it's best to say the things that come into my mind. The man I'm involved with—I find it very strange that he often pees sitting down. I think it's not very manly. He says, *That way I can talk to whoever's in the room!* But it's very weird that he does that. I don't know why I'm connecting that to your story, but there's something about a person whose back is turned . . . because your boyfriend is wanting to be connected to you—he's sticking his connection things out, but yours are only going to be present if you're connected to yourself. So I think the central method of improving your relationship is to connect it to yourself on a very deep level.

Okay . . .

And . . . I think I see a pregnant belly again. Why do I keep seeing . . . ? You've talked about maybe wanting to have a child. And it seems fine if you do, and it seems fine if you don't. But this whole reading is about doing the work of stepping over a gigantic wall—and you have to find out what that transformation is for you. I think maybe you're wanting the transformation to be pregnancy—you're talking about the happiness of the pregnancy—yet from everything I've seen about having a baby, once the baby arrives, it's not the joyride it looks like.

Now, this card is Death—your first Major Arcana. It is the burning of the phoenix, the burning of the blood. You know, our creativity is connected very deep into our soul, it's our very deepest, most central energy. I painted and painted, and then I did a portrait commission business, and then one day I fell down on the floor and I couldn't do it anymore. Because here's my heart-center, and then I start connecting it to paying my public utilities bill, and then some fucking jerk comes over and says, *But that isn't my son's nose!* Is there any chance that your art form is bleeding you out?

Perhaps?

Well, hon, I think you're in for a big burning—and you have to let it happen. You need to make a concentrated effort, and really fall into that deep space.

But will it destroy my life?

No, no! It's not going to destroy your life. Don't worry. It's not going to destroy your life at all. Now, this is the Moon card. This shows that it *does* go back to that painful place of your mom being depressed. The Moon card is about what's hidden inside—something that's causing you pain, blocking your relationship, blocking your art, and blocking your own peace. This card is almost asking, Can you look into that corner of your life? Can you say, *I'm going to walk into that moon quadrant of me that I don't know.* That whole idea of walking in, looking around, and just letting it be the truth. *What is the truth of this single quadrant of me?* It's just one part! The part that no one sees.

And your final outcome card is . . . Seven of Pentacles! That's a good final outcome card! It means, *I'm starting over with something great and new.* Look at what you're going to produce! Glowing, beautiful pieces of fruit—or whatever those things are. And the light is shining through them. That pink light is gorgeous, just *gorgeous!* Maybe there can be something beautiful that happens with the bleeding out.

I walked back through the streets and returned to my hotel room, where I went immediately to the washroom, and saw that I had been bleeding on my nice white underwear, as I suspected.

You can become accustomed to anything in this life, but blood coming out of your vagina once a month is nothing. I think, *Isn't it stupid my body did this again? Will it never learn? Will it never take the hint?* No, it replies: *Will* you *never take the hint?* If I paid more attention to the bleeding, maybe I would. But I don't: I deal with it, and it goes. Will I miss it one day, once it's gone for good? Why is my body doing this inside me every month, and how many opportunities could I miss? How stupid am I really? How little I care for what it wants. How neglected and abandoned is this little animal inside me that is doing its work so diligently and well—this tiny uterus, these mushy ovaries, these fallopian tubes and my brain. It has no idea I need nothing from it. It just keeps on working. If only I could speak to it and tell it to stop. Who is it doing all this for, if not for me? And what do I do for *it?* I mop up its blood. Then I mop it up again. I never feel grateful. I never give a single thought to each expectant egg—hopeful when ovulating, then saddened when I don't get pregnant and it's released from my body, confused as a girl who no one calls, who no boy ever asks out, who no one ever invites to a party. Then one day, the school finds out: She's dead. *What? That girl we all ignored?* Yes.

Miles once told me that I bleed less on my period than any other woman he's been with. With other women, whenever they would have sex during her period, the blood would be halfway up his belly and halfway down his thighs. With me, there's hardly a spot.

I wonder if it means I have a very small uterus, I said, the one time he told me this.

He just shrugged. To him, it didn't mean anything. Yet for an hour after, I hung suspended between the thought that I must be a truly refined woman to bleed much less, and I must not be much of a woman at all.

Heading home from that village, it felt as though never in my life had I realized how uncomfortable people made me. Every person on the train made me feel inferior, shy and confused— battered and awkward. When an older man smiled at me, it felt important not to look at him. A group of men seemed very interested in two sisters. When one took her hair down, it fell to just above her shoulders, and she was even more beautiful than she had been before. Then she put her hair back up. She was wearing sneakers and a leather jacket and jeans. The sisters were wearing make-up, yet there was something masculine about them, too. Their lips were bright and prettily shaped.

I thought about how city life was only one form of life, and how the structures we make are static and not all that complex. They do not shimmer like the dry grasses on the hills or the leaves on the trees. There are not as many examples in the city of the impossibly far and the impossibly close. In the country, there is the closeness of the grass as you lay down on it, and the vast expanse of the sea stretching up to the sky. In the city, everything is of equal significance, from everything being so equally close up. True perspective is pretty much impossible. The buildings do not sway in the wind, so it's harder for our ideas to sway. You cannot look at a building for several hours, while in nature you can look at anything for several hours, because nature is alive and ever-changing.

FOLLICULAR

Barcelona was governed in the Middle Ages by an oligarchy of nobles, merchants, shopkeepers and artisans, who formed the Council of One Hundred. This council had to answer to the king, but the king did not rule absolutely. He was seen to rule by contract and not by divine right. The leaders of the council swore him this oath: *We, who are as good as you, swear to you, who are no better than us, to accept you as our king and sovereign, provided you observe all of our liberties and laws—but if not, not.*

From that, R. B. Kitaj took the title of his painting of Auschwitz, *If Not, Not*. What is this idea of *not not?*

Are you going to have a child? If I do, I do—and if not, not. I . . . who am as good as you . . . will accept you . . . provided you observe . . . all of our liberties. And I don't want 'not a mother' to be part of who I am—for my identity to be the negative of someone else's positive identity. Then maybe instead of being 'not a mother' I could be *not 'not a mother.'* I could be *not not.*

If I am *not not*, then I am what I am. The negative cancels out the negative and I simply am. I am what I positively am, for the *not* before the *not* shields me from being simply *not* a mother. And to those who would say, *You're not a mother*, I would reply, 'In fact, I am not *not* a mother.' By which I mean I am *not 'not a mother.'* Yet someone who is called a mother could also say, 'In fact, I am not not a mother.' Which means she is a mother, for the *not* cancels out the *not*. To be *not not* is what the mothers can be, and what the women who are not mothers can be. This is the term we can share. In this way, we can be the same.

~

Tonight, I was reading a story about the Baal Shem Tov—one of the holy rabbis of the eighteenth century—and in the story, the Baal Shem Tov's daughter asks her father to tell her the name of the man she will marry, and to say whether she will ever be a mother. Her father throws a party and at the party her husband is revealed to her. The story ends by saying that she had two boys and one girl, and the names of the boys are given, and what they grew up to be, but the name of the daughter is not given, nor what she grew up to be (presumably a mother). Putting the book down, I realized that throughout most of history, it was enough for men that women existed to give birth to men and raise them. And if a woman gave birth to a girl, well then, with luck the girl would grow up to give birth to a man. It seemed to me like all my worrying about not being a mother came down to this history—this implication that a woman is not an end in herself. She is a means to a man, who will grow up to be an end in himself, and do something in the world. While a woman is a passageway through which a man might come. I have always felt like an end in myself—doesn't everyone?—but perhaps my doubt that being an end-in-myself is enough comes from this deep lineage of women not being seen as ends, but as passageways through which a man might come. If you refuse to be a passageway, there is something wrong. You must at least *try*.

But I don't want to be a passageway through which a man might come, then manifest himself in the world however he likes, without anyone doubting his right.

~

There are squirrels in the walls, or mice there. As I write, I can hear them moving, chewing the insides of the walls. I can hear them scratch on the insides of the walls, their little teeth chewing. They are eating the insulation, or wood, or cement, or whatever is in these walls.

~

If I consider raising a child in my own home and say this is what I have chosen *not* to do, what have I chosen, if anything? Language doesn't fit around this experience. It is therefore not an experience we can speak of. But I want a word that is utterly independent of the task of child-rearing, with which to think about this decision—a word about what *is*, and not what is not.

But how do you describe the absence of something? If I refuse to play soccer, is my not playing soccer an experience of playing soccer? My lack of the experience of motherhood is not an experience of motherhood. Or is it? Can I call it a motherhood, too?

What is the main activity of a woman's life, if not motherhood? How can I express the absence of this experience, without making central the lack? Can I say what such a life is an experience of *not* in relation to motherhood? Can I say what it *positively* is? Of course, it's different for every woman. Then can I say what it positively is for me? I cannot. Because I'm still in a place of indecision, not knowing what I want. I haven't yet birthed the person who by actively choosing not to have children lives in a way that positively affirms non-parental values, nor can I affirm the maternal experience of life.

Maybe if I could somehow figure out what *not having a child* is an experience of—make it into an active action, rather than the lack of an action—I might know what I was experiencing, and not feel so much like I was waiting to act. I might be able to choose my life, and hold in my hands what I have chosen, and show it to other people, and call it mine.

~

I always felt jealous of the gay men I knew who spoke of having come out. I felt I would like to come out, too—but as what? I could never put my finger on it. I had ghost images of the sort of person I was like, and ghost images of the sort of person I was not like. I wanted to be able to say of myself—*I have known this about myself since I was six years old. Some people were very condemning of me, but now I feel much better. I feel so much better since having come out. My life is now truly my own.*

~

I fear that without children, it doesn't look like you have made a choice, or that you're doing anything but just continuing on— drifting. People who don't have children might be thought not to move forward, or change and grow, or have stories that build on stories, or lives of ever-increasing depth and love and pain. Maybe they seem stalled in one place—a place the parents have left behind.

What is chosen by those who don't want children often looks no different from what the parents lived—just a continuation of what they lived before. It looks no different from not having procreated *yet*. It can look like getting ready to choose, or even like you're trying for a child. Yet there is a positive thing that is being lived and chosen by those who don't want children. But how can we say what that is, when parents feel they have lived it too, and that they know it well? Yet many of them lived it without choosing it, or lived it while knowing it was going to end.

~

Some people try to imagine what it's like not to have children— and they imagine themselves without children, instead of picturing a person they might never be. They project their own potential sadness over not having this experience on those who don't want it at all. A person who can't understand why someone doesn't want children only has to locate their feelings for children, and imagine that desire directed somewhere else—to a life that is just as filled with hope, purpose, futurity and care.

Why don't we understand some people who don't want children as those with a different, perhaps biologically different, orientation? Wanting not to have children could even be called a sexual orientation, for what is more tied to sex than the desire to procreate or not? I suspect the intensity of this desire lies deep within our cells, and then there is all that culture adds, and that other people add, which skews our innate desires. I can look back at being a tiny child and see that I did not want children then. I remember sitting at the kitchen table with my entire family, and suddenly knowing that I would never be a mother, for I was a *daughter*—*existentially*—and I always would be.

~

I know that Jewish women are expected to repopulate from the losses of the Holocaust. *If you don't have children, the Nazis will have won.* I have felt this. *They wanted to wipe us from the earth, and we must never let them.* Then how can I imagine *not* having children, and selfishly contribute to our dying out? Yet, I don't really care if the human race dies out.

Rather than repopulating the world, might it not be better to say, *We have learned from our history about the farthest reaches of cruelty, sadism and evil. And so, in protest, we will make no more people—no more people for a hundred years!—in retaliation for the crimes that were committed against us. We will make no more aggressors, and no more victims, and in this way, do a good thing with our wombs.*

I went out for dinner last night with my high school friend Libby. She recently found out that she was pregnant, and has not had one moment of joy with the idea. Her relationship had not been a serious one, but now it suddenly was. They had started looking for a condo. As she talked, I saw how it would be a trap—how the child could trap her with her new boyfriend, in a new life. Already the architecture was rising around her, like the growth of a city, sped-up. Skyscrapers were flying up; a new boyfriend, a new baby, new in-laws, a new home. The walls are being erected outside her as her baby grows inside her.

~

Every time I hear that a friend is having a baby, I feel like I'm being cornered by a looming force, more trapped still. You know the babies cannot keep coming forever, but for now they are raining down as heavy as night-hail, or whatever hits the earth and makes a crater sized so much bigger than the thing itself that hit it. There are craters, craters, all around, and no home is safe enough not to be pummelled to dust by these blessings, by these bits of stardust, these thousand-pound babies aimed straight at the earth.

I had always thought my friends and I were moving into the same land together, a childless land where we would just do a million things together forever. I thought our minds and souls were all cast the same way, not that they were waiting for the right moment to jump ship, which is how it feels as they abandon me here. I should not think of it as an abandoning, but it would be wrong to say it's not a loss, or that I'm not startled at being so alone. How had I taken all of us as the same? Is that why I started wondering about having kids—because, one by one, the ice floe on which we were all standing was broken and made smaller, leaving me alone on just the tiniest piece of ice, which I had thought would remain vast, like a very large continent on which we'd all stay? It never occurred to me that I'd be the only one left here. I know I'm not the only one left, yet how can I trust the few who remain, when I'd been so mistaken about the rest? I'm shaken by their wholesale deserting. Did they ever intend to stay on this childless continent, and then they changed their minds? Or had they never intended to stay, and I understood them all wrong?

I resent the spectacle of all this breeding, which I see as a turning away from the living—an insufficient love for the rest of us, we billions of orphans already living. These people turn with open arms to a new life, hoping to make a happiness greater than their own, rather than tending to the already-living. It's not right, it's not kind, when everyone you look at is a crying baby, and there my friends go, making more—making another one!—another new light in the world. Certainly I am *happy* for them, but I am miserable for the rest of us—for that absolute kick in the teeth, that relieved and joyful desertion. When a person has a child, they are turned towards their child. The rest of us are left in the cold.

OVULATING

Returning from the shower in a towel this morning, I found Miles standing in the middle of the bedroom, getting dressed. Then he smiled and danced his fingers and sang the song of the two birds who love me.

Last week, he bought me the most beautiful coat, and these tulips on the nightstand, and he cooks dinner for me, and last month when I was in bed sick he bought me three chocolate bars, and six bottles of sparkling water, and herbal cough medicine, and real cough medicine, and he drew many fat hearts on the wall beside the bed. I can't help but say it, but I feel I have found my true love.

Last night we had sex. It seems to always be the case that on the day I ovulate, Miles wants to fuck me. Somehow his body can always tell.

Marie Stopes, a birth control reformer from the early twentieth century, wrote that heterosexual couples had sex all wrong: their timing accorded to the regular rhythms of male body, not the fluctuating rhythms of the female. She said it should be timed with the woman's body: during the week of ovulation, couples should have sex daily, or several times a day, then refrain for the rest of the month. Those weeks of abstinence will build up longing, and let the couple focus on other tasks. I once proposed this to Miles as a good idea we try, and he agreed, but we never did.

Having sex half-asleep in the middle of the night, I got scared that Miles might accidentally come in me. It suddenly felt like a prison sentence—a terrible thing that would befall us, no going back, not what I wanted, the draining of all hope. I saw both of us with our dreams crushed.

I have done so many things to avoid it—including one abortion, several instances of the morning-after pill, and only choosing men who didn't want kids, or at least never being with a man who really did.

Besides, there are so many kinds of life to give birth to in this world, apart from a literal human life. And there are children everywhere, and parents needing help everywhere, and so much work to be done, and lives to be affirmed that are not necessarily the lives we would have chosen, had we started again. The whole world needs to be mothered. I don't need to invent a brand new life to give the warming effect to my life I imagine mothering will bring. There are lives and duties everywhere just crying out for a mother. That mother could be you.

~

The hardest thing is actually *not* to be a mother—to refuse to be a mother to anyone. To not be a mother is the most difficult thing of all. There is always someone ready to step into the path of a woman's freedom, sensing that she is not yet a mother, so tries to make her into one. There will always be one man or another, or her mother or her father, or some young woman or some young man who steps into the bright and shimmering path of her freedom, and adopts themselves as that woman's child, forcing her to be their mother. Who will knock her up this time? Who will emerge, planting their feet before her, and say with a smile, *Hi mom!* The world is full of desperate people, lonely people and half-broken people, unsolved people and needy people with shoes that stink, and socks that stink and are holey—people who want you to arrange their vitamins, or who need your advice at every turn, or who just want to talk and get a drink—and seduce you into being their mother. It's hard to detect this is even happening, but before you realize it—it's happened.

~

The most womanly problem is not giving oneself enough space or time, or not being allowed it. We squeeze ourselves into the moments we allow, or the moments that have been allowed us. We do not stretch out in time, languidly, but allot ourselves the smallest parcels of time in which to exist, miserly. We let everyone crowd us. We are miserly with our selves when it comes to space and time. But doesn't having children lead to the most miserly allotment of space and time? Having a child solves the impulse to give oneself nothing. It makes that impulse into a virtue. To feed oneself last in self-abnegation, to fit oneself into the smallest spaces in the hopes of being loved—that is entirely womanly. To be virtuously miserly towards oneself in exchange for being loved—having children gets you there fast.

I want to take up as much space as I can in time, stretch out and stroll with nowhere to go, and give myself the largest parcels of time in which to do nothing—to let my obligations slip to the ground, reply to no one, please no one, leave everyone hanging, impolitely, and try to win no one's favor; not pile up politenesses doled out to just everyone in the hopes of being pleasing, so I won't be thrown out of society as I fear I will be, if I don't live like a good maid, gingerly.

I get nostalgic for being a teenager for this reason. It never occurred to me then to be nice to other people. I look back at that time as a time of great freedom—but *that* was the great freedom, that I didn't give a fuck. I cannot give a fuck more than I already do. I feel it would be the end of me. Having children is *nice*. What a great victory to be *not-nice*. The nicest thing to give the world is a child. Do I ever want to be that nice?

PMS

Weeks have passed, and the tears, once again, are back. What am I supposed to do with my unhappiness? Is it like the fortune teller said: these tears were planted in me before I was born?

yes

Should I love them?

no

Accept them?

no

Try and work them out?

yes

By writing?

yes

Why? To overcome?

yes

Is my sadness related to the demon in my dreams?

yes

Then the thing to do is keep wrestling. I must ask for the demon-angel's blessing, and understand how dependent I am. If I recognize my dependence, truly and deeply, will the bad feelings go away?

no

No, but at least I'll be sitting in the truth?

yes.

~

Libby and I met for dinner last night. As the evening wore on, she became more and more upset with me. She expressed anxiety about me moving forward in my work, while she said she was falling behind in hers. With her pregnancy-brain, she felt sure she would fall behind everyone she knew and never work or make anything ever again. She was so upset. She told me not to do so much. *Stop making things!* she said.

When later I told Miles what she had said, he was unsurprised. *You see? It's not benign—this pressure your women friends are putting on you to have kids. They want you to be in the same boat they're in. They want you to have the same handicap they have.* He reiterated that it wasn't worth it—parenthood. He called it *the biggest scam of all time.*

Libby was so frightening last night. She said she was losing her mind. I disagreed, but I could see it, and I grew frightened, too. I saw how she might change for good—become even a little less like the person I had known. She said her brain was being wiped clean so she could learn to love a new person. She said this is what happens when people are pregnant, or when they fall in love—it's like they get amnesia, so new pathways can be created. She spoke to me from a dream within a dream, and said such horrible things. *Stop making things! You keep making things!* she cried. Her body was making something, she admitted, but *she* was not. I said that I wasn't making anything, but she did not believe me.

All the next day, I lay in bed with the blinds shut, despairing and numb. I didn't rise till dark. Until that dinner, there had been no sign of a change in her. I suppose I had been living in a fantasy. Maybe we both had been. I couldn't tell her what I'd seen. I felt she needed to push *me* out of her heart, so there would be more room for her child to grow.

I feel terrible today—so tired. The day started off with a fight, with Miles seemingly ignoring me. When he does that, I feel like he's trying to prove that he does not love me. Then I cried, then he got angry. Then I went for a walk and felt bad in the streets, then I came home and felt bad here. Now I'm sitting at my desk, and I'm still feeling bad. It's going to be a long day of bad feelings. I feel so worn out and wretched, like I do whenever we fight. Just remember: you will never remember the sadness you are feeling right now. You will never even remember it. It will be like all the other moments of your life—gone. And the evening, too, is already almost gone.

There is nothing new about this time. There is nothing new about the fact that our lives will not turn out the way we supposed. There is nothing new about the fact that the great dreams we had for our lives will not turn into our actual lives.

It's sometimes so hard to understand what I'm doing in this life, because I'm living for such strange things. Maybe we are capable of making the right choices, before we fully understand the reasons. I must accept that my choices are the right ones, but for mysterious reasons. Or perhaps they are the wrong choices, but for the right reasons. Yet we do not live for *the right reasons*, we live for our own reasons. When we figure out what those reasons are, our choices will all make sense.

In my dream last night, I heard the words, *If you want to know what your life is, destroy everything and move away and see what builds up again. If what builds up a second time is much the same as the first, then your life is pretty much as it could be. Things couldn't be much different from that.*

~

I know there is no difference between someone with children and someone without—that having a child or not is just part of what happened to them, or what time and the world made happen to them, and of course they are part of the world, and so is the person they are with, and the person they are not with, and their culture, and their parents, and their work, and their bodies, and how much money they earn, and the baby who came or didn't come or died. The world isn't as binary for me as it was before, with parents on one side, and non-parents on the other. Seeing someone with a child tells me nothing about the life that was in their head, or is currently in their head, just as seeing someone without a child tells me nothing about the life that was in *their* head. Life occurs to each of us, equally, with all its forces of randomness and care, and whatever forces act on a human life, which we can only guess at but still don't know.

Then don't ask questions about things that could go either way. The reason you can't find an answer, whenever you can't, is because the answer doesn't much matter, in the general course of things. If something can be debated endlessly and without resolution, it *cannot* matter. The things that cannot be debated are the things that matter most. For some, it cannot be debated whether they will have a child, but for those for whom it *can* be debated, it's probably a fine life either way. Then if it doesn't matter to you, and it doesn't matter to the world, do what is better for the world, and don't have one.

There is no inherent good in being born. The child would not otherwise miss its life. Nothing harms the earth more than another person—and nothing harms a person more than being born. If I really wanted to have a baby, it would be better to adopt. Even better would be to give the money I would have spent on raising a child to those organizations that give women who can't afford it condoms and birth control and education and abortions, and so save these women's lives. That would be a more worthwhile contribution to this world than adding one more troubled person from my own troubled womb.

~

Sometimes I think that in not wanting children, I'm preparing for my old age. I know what I want my old age to look like, more than I know almost anything else: a simple home, a simple life, no one needing me for anything, and not needing anyone the way I do now. If a person has children, there is worry till death. Or jealousy over their young lives—someone to compare yourself to. As my mother once said to me, about me, *No one else makes me feel so old.*

~

When my mother was a little girl, she dreamed of being a florist, a photographer, or a figure skater, but her mother made her go to university to become a professional woman. It is not so strange to live the dreams of one's parents, if their dreams are somehow prevented.

I remember being a little girl and my mother showing me slides through her heavy, metal microscope: blood and liver, kidneys, the heart. The slides were dyed purple and pink, and revealed all the beautiful patterns of nature, not unlike the unfolding of the flowers she loved, or the circles cut into ice by a figure skater's turns. She would sit at the dining-room table with her slides spread out around her, then she'd stand me on the chair and lead my eyes in close to the eyepiece to see. She would say, *This is your blood.* It was amazing to me that those little, separate donuts, each one tender in its own way, and each one shaped slightly differently from the other ones, was the truth of my blood. Then she would pluck out one of my hairs and put it under the microscope. *And this is your hair.* Could that hollow reed be the truth of my hair? My mother could see to the smallest parts of everything. There was power in how my mother could see.

~

In the far distance, I can hear the banging of a hammer, children's voices and a woman's voice. The winter sun shines in. Overhead, there's an airplane. A bird in a tree makes a demanding squawk, then a few gentler ones. The days are getting crisp.

Miles, in the bathroom, bangs things in the sink. A car parks outside my window and I can hear it idling. Miles sings lightly as he walks down the hall, then he clears his voice: *Oh, sorry.*

Are you working? In a moment I'm going to go into the hall and say goodbye to him for the day. I can hear him opening and closing his drawers. The car is still idling, the hammer is still hammering. The floorboards creak beneath his feet.

In my dream last night, there were many women nearing the end of their childbearing years, all hanging around with each other on sofas, together. They were beautiful and alluring, but they didn't have much in the way of men or children, and this was at once their power and their independence, and their loss and their shallowness, their lightness and their emptiness.

Many people barter with their conditions. They suspect if they willingly give something up—something they desire—the universe, in recompense, will make up for the loss. But the universe does not play tradesies, and often what is lost is gone for good.

Will I be one of those women, who, at forty, suddenly wants a baby? No one wants to be one of those women—to realize what you want when it's practically too late. Who wants to be seen by the world as having been wrong about such a basic thing? Yet the threat of this hangs over me like an anvil that will fall on my head to the laughter of all. You are thirty-nine. People decide now. Even my doctor agreed: *you have to decide now.*

I know that forty is just an idea in the mind—a finish line that isn't one. Yet I crave a finish line, just to stop thinking about this. When I hear about women having babies over forty, I feel a sinking in my chest. Won't this time-period ever end?

Why this constant oscillation? How can one week it seem like such a good idea—and the next week it seems so wrong? How much has my deliberation won me in terms of the path of my life? Desire stems not from deliberating over what you want—it comes from someplace deeper. You can't make something come that at the same time you don't want. That push and pull creates nothing. It will continue to create nothing for all of time. Anywhere in your life where there is push and pull—look away from it to someplace else, to where the energy is going in one direction. Find your way into that stream and propel your life from there.

The problem is that life is long, and so much happens by accident, and choices made in a single week can affect an entire lifetime, and the decider within us is not always under our control. So as much as I can't see having a child, it's strange to imagine I actually won't. Yet the not-having seems just as amazing, unlikely and special as the having. Both feel like a kind of miracle. Both seem like a great feat. To go along with what nature demands and to resist it—both are really beautiful—impressive and difficult in their own ways. To battle nature and to submit to nature, both feel very worthy. They both seem entirely valuable.

~

I feel too tired to keep writing this—drained, depressed, worn through. Thinking about children weakens my fingers, and puts me in a deep sleep, like smelling a potent flower. There are all sorts of gates to the truth. Sleepiness is one. I must fight to the other side of this exhaustion, this strange sleepiness, and know for myself what I want.

The question of a child is a bug in the brain—it's a bug that crawls across everything, every memory, and every sense of my own future. How to dislodge that bug? It's eating holes in everything there ever was or will be. Nothing remains intact.

How much of me thinks that my problems—whatever vagueness is associated with living—would be solved by stuffing my days with childcare, and my heart with my own child, instead of being only half an animal in the eyes of the world? This is not a good feeling to carry around in one's life. It can feel as though the solution to everything is just to give in to the part of me that *wants* to do this simple thing that opens and lifts the heart.

~

Some part of me knows that these are the years I'm supposed to have a child. Sometimes when I think about it, I can feel a pleasant anticipation and a succumbing, like there's little in life left to do. A space has opened up inside of every molecule of an instant, where I can see a child would go. But I am not capable of putting a child there. I don't know how to get a child into those molecules of time.

The other night I had a dream which said it was good to keep walking down the very same streets; that the longer I walked down them, the more I would find. *Slowing down is important*, said the dream. *Repetition important. Be in the same place, differently. Change the self, not the place.*

~

It's true that a person can for so long twiddle her thumbs and call it work—call anything work but what's truly work. To be honestly quiet, and work in true quietude—to write about things that actually deserve one's attention. Which are what?

All I want to do is sit and stare at a watermelon all day. To rock a watermelon in my arms. Sing it songs, lug it around. All I want is to fall asleep, and sleep for a million years. Or maybe I want to have a baby—but with someone who really wants it—wants it and wants it with me. Or else to find out whether I really want a child by being with another man and seeing. With Miles, I will never know what I want, his own wants being so strong. I need to be farther from his preferences, in order to know my own.

~

I wonder if all of my thinking about having children is connected to losing faith in the bigger ideas—art, politics, romance. Child-rearing is not abstract, like making art or trying to change the world. Perhaps as you get older and are more in the world, the less you care to change it.

Then maybe it is cynical for me to think of having children. Maybe it reflects a cynicism about literature—after having seen what happens to art in the world—how something you love becomes dirty, and you become dirty, too. Maybe this is what happens with children, also, which is perhaps partly why people want to have more than one. The baby's perfect innocence and purity is gone, corrupted as they grow. The same thing happens with art. It starts off in a state of perfect innocence, and you along with it. Then it becomes corrupted as it moves through the world, and you do, too.

All this wondering about children is just evidence of how much a person can give up what they know is right. It would be easier to have a child than to do what I want. Yet when I so frequently do the opposite of what I want, what is one more thing? Why not go all the way into falsehood, for me? I might as well have kids. Yet that is where I draw the line. You can't create a person dishonestly. At least I have that bit of morality going for me—that bit of right action. Raising children is the opposite of everything I long for, the opposite of everything I know how to do, and all the things I enjoy.

How not to give up all your ideals as you move through life. But also, how it's okay to change.

~

Is it immoral to have babies, because that is trapping the immortal soul in a mortal body?
no
Is it *good* to trap the immortal soul inside a mortal body?
yes
So that the immortal soul can learn?
yes
Does it sometimes happen that an immortal soul, trapped inside a human body, goes backwards; becomes more ignorant?
yes
Is the immortal soul shared by all of humankind?
yes

So if the immortal soul in me learns, does the immortal soul in another person learn, too?

yes

And if the immortal soul becomes more ignorant in another, it also does in me. Then it really matters what we do. Is it possible that someone has a baby, and this having a baby makes them more ignorant, whereas not having a baby would have made them more wise?

yes

Would that be the case with me—that in having a child, my soul would become more ignorant?

no

Would my soul become more wise?

no

Stay pretty much the same?

yes.

~

I know the more I think about having a child, the more that creates the figure of the child who is not born. The more I write this, the more this not-born child becomes a real thing, a figure *not there*, a specific person who is being denied life. Perhaps in this negative way, that child will live. That child will live as its opposite: the never-born child. Or perhaps all of this writing will compel me to have a child, having summoned him or her in this way—summoned him by repeatedly denying him. Or maybe it will create a child whose reality in language will be enough.

Writing seems so small in comparison to motherhood. It doesn't feel like it will fill up all the nooks and crannies of the soul. And perhaps it won't. But even if one is a mother, are all the nooks and crannies filled up?

~

I remember being twenty and seeing several writers on a literary panel on stage—both women and men. They said that of course writing was important to them, but their children were much more important than that. I felt so put off. They seemed so unserious to me. I never wanted to be like that—to have something in my life that was more important than writing. Why would they do that to themselves?

But in the years that followed, my fear changed: could I ever hope to be a good enough writer—capture on the page what being human felt like—if I had not experienced motherhood? If I had no experience of what I increasingly took to be the central experience of life?

~

Last night, some friends came over and things got quite grim. One friend said that in her forties, a woman suddenly sees all she could have done and all the ways she could have lived if she had not made her life so dependent on a man.

Another said, *All I have left now is my integrity*. She had married at forty, and she so much wanted it to work, even though she knew the man wasn't her soulmate. But she wanted a child. So they married quickly, and had a baby, then two years later, they divorced. Her mother once asked her, *Would you rather have a soulmate or would you rather have a child?* She told her mother that she wanted both.

I thought about the question for a moment. I would rather have a soulmate, speaking honestly.

~

When Miles's daughter comes to stay, I remind myself to be careful: her visits are not evidence of what it would be like to have a child who would not be *her,* and who would be mothered by me, not her own mother, who has not indifferently dedicated her life to her care. What could be more unlike motherhood than *this*—that she always returns to her mother? This is the part that has always frightened me most—the endlessness of motherhood, its eternity. Seeing someone pushing a baby in a stroller, I always feel a profound exhaustion: *But there are so many years still to go!*

I feel I don't have a good enough reason to make someone live and work and pay for their days, and suffer for eighty-odd years. You can't make someone live to resolve a debate in your mind, or because you are curious for every human experience, or to fit in with your friends. I could only give a child a worse life than I was given. How do people have the confidence to ever think otherwise?

Erica once said, *We had our child as a hedge against future regret.* But is it right to make someone live, so you might not feel some regret?

Unlike Erica, I have always feared that I would regret having had one, more than regret *not* having—for it has not escaped my notice that my happy imaginings of being a mother are always about *having* mothered—of smiling and waving at the front door as the children move on.

I just read over a journal from a year ago and it could have been written today. NOTHING but NOTHING has changed! How maddening! After years of thinking about whether I want a baby, and writing hundreds of thousands of words thinking about it, I am in pretty much the same place, my feelings about it more or less unchanged; reason, thought, examining my desires, has brought me no closer to knowing.

It sometimes seems as if the question of having children can only be resolved one way—by having them. For even if one comes to a definite resolution *against* having children, hanging over one's head remains a spectre, the possibility, that a child will come. Or that life circumstances will conspire to make you change your mind, and if not actually bring about children, then make you regret not having had them.

Yet I have to think, *If I wanted a kid, I already would have had one by now—or at least I would have tried.* For how long am I expected to live as though there is a second me, hiding somewhere inside? When will it finally feel safe to prioritize the *me* I know?

I need to force myself to see things in a new way. It's time, for god's sake! I set myself up for so much misery. Imagine the questions of someone else, someone with a broader mind— then try to *be* that broader mind. Don't ask yourself questions you don't want the answers to, just like how Miles told me that he didn't ask the man who was selling us the chairs *why* he was selling them, because he didn't think he'd like the answer. That man was such a good man, such a likeable, warm and endearing man, in his tiny white apartment, with pictures of his children on all the walls, and signs on every cupboard and door, *THINK OF THE POSITIVE.*

~

I can remember—but barely—a time before I thought about having children so much—when the future was uncontaminated by the possibility of a child, or uncontaminated by the loss of not having had one. Erica said that it seems like I actually *do* want a child. Do I?

no

Why are you saying I don't? Because you think you know anything at all?

yes

What do you know? Do you know my insides?

yes

Can you even remember what you answered, from one question to the next?

yes

Is all of this even *writing*?

no

Randomness is useless and leads nowhere! It is better to believe nothing than to believe things randomly and haphazardly. It is better to have a foundation from which to rule one's behaviour and life, than this randomness and haphazardness, which leads as much to absurdity as it does to anything true. It is only fear that makes us interrogate too deeply into our relationships, and only a lust for power that makes us interrogate too deeply into the unknown. Nothing worth knowing can be known, and feelings, which fluctuate constantly, cannot be the things that guide us through life, which is designed to make feelings fluctuate so. We are dependent on each other and we all need so much. What matters is to overcome—to erase the boundary between the spiritual and the physical, and finally become whole. We must ask the demon for its blessings, and forget about the rest.

~

The man who was selling us the chairs—his apartment had almost nothing in it—white walls, few things. As Miles was putting the chairs in the car, the man told me that he wouldn't accept a new pair of shoes if he already had one pair. He saw other people striving to build up their lives, moving to bigger cities, building admirable careers, buying cars and furnishings, cultivating grand connections and friends. *Desires build up lives*, he warned. He feared that if he began to follow his desires, he would end up buried underneath whatever they collected, until his whole self disappeared.

There must be, in the puzzle of desires, some who wait out their days, and some who desire nothing at all. Some people want to fill up their entire lives, while others want to empty them out—to shake them until everything inessential falls out.

What is your motivation? I asked him. He said, *I don't have a motivation. I live a very simple life. I do my work. After dinner, I sleep. I have no interest in having adventures.*

~

In the car ride home, Miles said, *Of course raising children is a lot of hard work, but I don't see why it's supposed to be so virtuous to do work that you created for yourself out of purely your own self-interest. It's like someone who digs a big hole in the middle of a busy intersection, and then starts filling it up again, and proclaims: Filling up this hole is the most important thing in the world I could be doing right now.*

~

I know the longer I work on this book, the less likely it is I will have a child. Maybe that is why I'm writing it—to get myself to the other shore, childless and alone. This book is a prophylactic. This book is a boundary I'm erecting between myself and the reality of a child. Perhaps what I'm trying to do in writing this is build a raft that will carry me just so long and so far, that my questions can no longer be asked. This book is a life raft to get me there. For myself, that's all it needs to be—not a great big ocean liner, just a barge. It can completely fall to pieces once I land on the other shore.

Now my periods are getting irregular. Even a year ago they came every twenty-eight days. Now they can be off by two days or three. It makes me sad to see this drop in my fitness to reproduce, and other things. Time is running out.

Time is always ticking for women. Whereas men, apparently, live in a timeless realm. In the dimension of men, there is no time—just space. Imagine living in the realm of space, not time! You put your dick into spaces, and the bigger your dick, the cozier the space. If you have a very big dick, then space—and life—must be very cozy indeed. Imagine having a very small dick—how vast and unknowable the universe must be to the small-dicked man! But if your dick is the size of most of what you encounter, nothing could be very threatening at all. For women, the problem is different. A fourteen-year-old girl has so much time to be raped and have babies that she is like the greatest Midas. The time-span of a woman's life is about thirty years. Apparently, during these thirty years—fourteen to forty-four—everything must be done. She must find a man, make babies, start and accelerate her career, avoid diseases, and collect enough money in a private account so that her husband can't gamble their life's savings away. Thirty years is not enough time to live a whole life! It's not enough time to do all of everything. If I have only done one thing with my time, this is surely what

I'll castigate myself for later. The day will come when I'll think, *What the fuck did you waste all those years putting in commas for?* I will have no idea how I could have been so naïve about how time acts in the life of a woman; how it is the essential realm in which a woman lives. All the things I neglected to do because I refused to believe, fundamentally, that first and foremost I was female.

You women who wish to live in the realm of space, not time—you will see what gifts the universe has waiting. *Will I?* Yes. Just look around. *But some women are happy!* But some women are not. *How do I know which I will be?* You cannot know until it's too late.

My mother told me, when I was a child, *You know that in my family the women were always the brains.* So I also wanted to be the brains: to be nothing but words on a page.

~

When I was growing up, my mother kept a framed photograph on the piano. It was the only photograph of her mother's family that survived. In the picture, Magda is twelve years old. She stands in a portrait studio with her parents and younger brothers. They are skinny and unsmiling. The family is so poor that the boys don't have shoes. The photographer had to paint shoes on the print: thin grey lines marking laces, eyeholes, leathers. My grandmother's face looks identical to mine. When I was twelve, and she was twelve, we could have been the same person.

When I was a child, part of me wondered, if our faces are so similar, what else about us might be similar? Are our minds, our feelings, identical, too? Who is to say that my grandmother's soul—in the fallow year between our lives—didn't reach into my body, and take up shelter there?

~

My mother could never please her mother: she was never smart enough for her mother, could never get good enough grades. She worked fifty times harder than anyone else. She let her mother's dreams become her own. She lived to please her mother, even once she was a mother, and even once her own mother had died. She lived her life turned towards her mother, not towards me.

~

How far beyond your mother do you hope to get? You are not going to be a different woman entirely, so just be a slightly altered version of her, and relax. You don't have to have all of what she had. Why not live something else, instead? Let the pattern which is the repeating, which was your mother, and her mother before her, live it a little bit differently this time. A life is just a proposition you ask it by living it, *Could a life be lived like this, too?*

Then your life will end. So let the soul that passed down from your mothers try out this new life in you. There is no living your life forever. It's just once—a trial of a life—then it will end. So give the soul that passed down from your mothers a chance to try out life in you.

As a custodian for the soul passed down through your mothers, you might make it a little easier for it this time around. Treat it nicely, because it's had a hard time. This is the first time in generations it can rest, or decide with true liberty what it will do. So why not treat it with real tenderness? It has been through so much already—why not let it rest?

Low tear count today, although the feeling of tears was in me yesterday. Still, there is a pressure, stretched-ness and dryness all around my eyes.

Someone cursed me, and my mother, and my mother's mother before me. The person who cursed us is now dead. It's a curse that turns me towards fixing my mother's sorrow, just as she was turned to fixing her mother's. My mother lived to fix the problem of her mother's life, given how Magda was cursed. I have taken on the curse as my own. We do not pursue happiness in marriage. We do not look for happiness with children. We think mainly of our work, to solve the problem of our mothers' tears.

My grandmother would not have wanted her daughter to be sad, and she would not have wanted her sadness to carry on through me. No one who has been through what she went through would have wanted her family to carry this sadness on.

~

I know only one other story about my grandmother's life in the camps. The women in Magda's barracks were told by a guard that the Germans were looking for female prisoners to help in the camp kitchen. They were told that anybody interested in volunteering should step forward. Magda stepped forward.

Everyone stepped forward, including a woman who Magda's future husband had dated prior to the war.

A German soldier yelled at my grandmother, *Not you*. He roughly hit her and she fell back from the group. The woman my grandfather had dated was chosen. Magda never saw her again. Later she learned that none of the women who stepped forward to volunteer were taken to a kitchen. They were all taken to the German army, raped by the soldiers, and then shot to death.

To have grown up knowing this story, I think gave me a strange feeling of the naturalness of family lines ending, as if our family line was supposed to end there, but it managed to slip by, but just barely—the way someone who has been shot might stumble forward a few more steps before collapsing dead. That is how my life has always felt to me: like those last few bloodied and hobbled steps after the bullet has pierced the body.

~

When I think about everything that could be or couldn't be, I think I don't want our flesh—my mother's flesh, my grandmother's flesh—to just be divided and replicated. I want their life to be counted. I want to make a child that will not die—a body that will speak and keep on speaking, which can't be shot or burned up. You can't burn every copy of a single book. A book is more powerful than any murderer, than any crime. Then to make a strong creature, stronger than any of us. To make a creature that lives inside many bodies, not just one body that is so vulnerable.

A book lives in every person who reads it. You can't just snuff it out. My grandmother got away from the camps. She got away so she could live. I want my grandmother to live in everybody, not just in one body from between my legs.

I do not feel I have the luxury to have a child. I do not have the time. My mother worked hard to justify her mother's life. She worked for her mother, to give meaning to her mother's life. She was turned towards her mother, not turned towards me. And I am turned towards my mother, too, and not towards any son or daughter. We turn our love backwards to make sense of life, to make beauty and significance of our mother's life.

Maybe motherhood means honoring one's mother. Many people do that by becoming mothers. They do it by having children. They do it by imitating what their mother has done. By imitating and honoring what their mother has done, this makes them a mother.

I also am imitating what my mother has done. I am also honoring my mother, no less than the person whose mother feels honored by an infant grandchild. I am honoring my mother no less. I do as my mother did, and for the same reasons; we work to give our mother's life meaning.

What's the difference between being a good mother and being a good daughter? Practically a lot, but symbolically nothing at all.

~

On the other hand, wouldn't my grandmother want us to be happy? Say, after our work was done? My mother retired this summer, after working nonstop and so hard all the way through school, from grade one until she retired in her late sixties. She achieved what she set out to do—the exact plan her mother put in place for her life. She should be at peace, happy—but she's not. Even though she did it—she fulfilled her destiny, and is now in its aftermath. She should be in heaven, free—if heaven is a place where your destiny is complete, and you are free of any destiny. There cannot be happiness when you are fulfilling a destiny. Happiness is the opposite. Happiness will have to wait.

BLEEDING

Today all I want to do is sob and leave everything. It's two days before my period, and I woke up in a fury, then Miles and I argued. I have a heart full of sadness and wishes. Everything feels like tears. *He* makes me feel like tears. But without a stress on the mind, there is no mind. Is what I am feeling the hormonal sadness?

yes

If only there was some good in it. Is there?

yes

Is the benefit that one stays away from other people?

yes

And one is also more sensitive. Both of these things are good for writing. I write more before my period than at any other time. I want to kill that ice cream truck with its odd, sad song! With its terrible, Portuguese song of tragedy. Will my sadness be gone by tomorrow night?

yes

It should have been gone already! It should have been gone yesterday, in fact. The fight with Miles prolonged it. Why do couples have so many problems with each other? Has anyone ever adequately answered this question?

yes

Was it a woman who did?

yes

Did a man give a good answer, too?

yes

Was the man's answer basically about blaming the woman?

yes

And did the woman's answer blame the man?

no

She blamed herself?

yes

Did the man blame the woman for her frailties?

yes

And did the woman just guiltily condemn herself?

yes

Would things work out better for men and women if women didn't just guiltily condemn themselves?

yes

I'm sorry. Are my frailties to blame?

yes.

~

I have been in a nervous panic all afternoon, not having heard from Miles. There is a trembling inside me, a feeling he will completely reject me, or that I don't know what's going on, or that he's mad. But why should his anger bother me, if I have done nothing wrong? Still, there is a deep panic inside.

There's a huge part of me that wants to please him, that feels I cannot, then gets angry when he doesn't show me what I feel is love. I wonder if it will get better, or if it can't be solved, and that as much as we care about each other, we won't be able to make it work. I feel sorry for all the men who came before him, whose feelings I didn't consider. I have a way of reducing the humanity of every man I'm with to a manageable size, and it's something I mustn't do.

I just feel so tired, so worn out from all our fighting. I think we might separate soon, and he'll go off without me. I just want to break it off because I can't stand the idea that this will happen out of my control. Yet I want him here at home to love me—not to be away! I want another man who will love me more. No, I only want him.

But what to do about this tremulous feeling inside?

~

I asked myself before falling asleep what I should do about my life, and when I woke in the middle of the night, this phrase accompanied me from my dream: *You need to control* yourself *if you are to have more meaning in your life.*

Easier said than done. He woke me up this morning by asking me what I wanted from St. Lawrence Market. I said a can of tomatoes. Then he got upset because he said he had made me tomato sauce a week ago and I had let it go to waste. After he left, I cried.

~

When Miles came in through the front door with groceries from the market, I saw that what was between us was real, and not a construction of my mind. I told him that things would be better from now on, but he didn't believe me. Also I know it's not true—I am powerless before my emotions. And I often want to retaliate against him for causing me so much pain.

There is no coming to consciousness without pain.

The pain that opens the door.

~

The simplest thing to do with pain is to deceive yourself into thinking it offers you an opportunity: by making it into a game, it becomes something less by which you suffer. By playing with it, you can turn it into the category of things you pick up, and can therefore put down. Thinking about your pain puts it in the category of the imaginary. But pain is not imaginary. It is wrong to think that the thoughtful escape it, or the very tricky, or the very wise. Those who skip town do not escape it, and those who skip between lovers do not. Drinking is no escape; gratitude lists are not. When you stop making a project of trying to escape your pain, it will still be there, but also a realization: that the pain is only as much as you can handle—like a glass of water filled to the brim, the water hovering at the meniscus, not running over.

~

Last night, I dreamed about three men—one representing Miles, one representing an ex-boyfriend, and one representing a man in New York. I saw my ex-boyfriend—and it felt simple between us, and there were no vetoes there. The New York one—I was told by an angel that this man was fine, but the angel had seen him cheating on girlfriends before, so he was dismissed. The angel said he had done his best in putting together Miles for me. I said there was friction, and he agreed: *Wasn't the friction good? The friction was a good part of the recipe.* I felt an intelligence up close to me, saying: *I have made this person for you. Why are you rejecting him?*

The question you must always ask is, *Is what I am suffering characteristic?* For there are pains that are characteristic, and pains that are uncharacteristic—characteristic suffering and uncharacteristic suffering, characteristic loneliness and uncharacteristic loneliness. Some suffering feels characteristic, it's deep and familiar in your bones. Other suffering feels alien, like it should not be happening to you.

What would be more characteristic for me: the suffering of being with Miles, or the suffering of being without Miles; the suffering of having children, or the suffering of being without? When I ask myself this question, the answer is clear: the suffering of being with Miles; the suffering of being without kids. We all know which suffering is meant to be ours. In every life, there is a quality of suffering. I have never before in any of my relationships felt such characteristic suffering as I do with Miles. With Miles, the suffering feels meaningful—like something of significance could be born.

It is true that he has cleared away so much somehow, and that I am down to the bare bones, the very roots of my existence, living so close to all the things that are most real and mine. I don't think it's anything he is consciously doing, or something I could point to. Maybe it's just finding something so endless.

~

I always believed there were several possible lives I could be living, and they were arranged in my head like dolls on a mantelpiece.

Daily I would take them down, one by one, dust them off, and examine their contours and compare. The life I was living felt no different from one of my doll-on-the-shelf lives, no different in plausibility or detail. I felt I could as easily be living one of those other lives as much as the life that was mine—and that if I was to make the decision to lead one of those lives, it would be as simple as swapping dolls.

How had I confused my life with a doll? It would have taken great force of reason—which I did not have—to convince me that even if I *was* to run away, it would be the exact same life—a continuation of this present one, and my same self in it. Those lives I pulled down from the shelf of my mind never contained the ashes of this present life, or the sorrow or consequences of deserting this one for that one, or any uncertainty about my new choice. But I did not think too deeply about any of this—it was just my obsession. I dusted and turned those other lives around, as if to give them up would be to give up my only security in the world, leaving me alone in the dark with nothing.

Happily we run away from even the brightest and best things in our lives, because we are curious about what else is out there. And what else is out there? Just more of the same, whichever way you look. Whichever way you turn, it's the same life you're facing. It's the same life that's facing you.

Miles never fantasizes about other lives, and he can't understand this part of me. *What a waste of time*, he once said. *If you're not actually going to do anything about it . . .*

But in some ways life is easier for him. It will always be easier for a man to know what he wants, and live his life accordingly. It is unfair of him to compare himself to me. Whenever I try to explain myself, he always says, *What's holding you back?* I cannot point to anything. What holds me back is my actual freedom— my reluctance before the void. Reluctant to make my own meanings, in case I make them up badly, afraid of being laughed at, a fool, apart. No one wants to be shunned. *There is only one place to live*, a great thinker once said, *and that is in civilization*.

Outside of civilization is where you get eaten by bears.

Always, having accepted that I want everything to change, I suddenly realise I do not. I want the dream of leaving, not leaving itself. The dream of other lives, not any other life. The trick is not to trick myself with too much dreaming, but to let my dreaming take me to the uttermost edges of desire and longing, without actually advancing too far—for my fantasies to only stretch so far, before snapping me back into my life.

~

I know Miles hates me right now. I could feel it in the air when I walked out the door, and I can feel it in the air, as I walk down the street. I want to resolve things and go home. But I don't think he's at home missing me. I think he's at home hating me. He says I don't care about him, which is wrong! He looks for evidence that I don't care, or regards my moods as proof that I don't. He regards my carelessness—which applies even to my own life—as proof that I don't value him, when I'm as careless with myself and my own property! I don't have a systematic way of doing things. I'm not thinking about the implications of everything, all of the time!

It's possible there is only one way out—through the exit. But I don't want to take this route. What if I look back and realise that

I was wrong; that Miles was not my tormentor, but my saviour? Perhaps I have to accept the great crashing of one planet into another, which is us, and the possibility that we will destroy each other. Or perhaps I have to change my approach—practice acceptance, quiet desperation, find joy in the situation and remain. The oracle said *follow truth*. But I can't speak the truth to him about anything! I grow moody instead, which he hates. The only way to leave would be with a steely heart—which is to say, without hope. But I love him, and am bonded to him—bound to him in so many ways, and I love to hold him—whatever parts of him come near, whenever they do, in their sweetness.

I have a hard time seeing both the good and the bad at once. Maybe *that* is the way forward: in every moment to see the good and the bad, rather than flipping back and forth. Sometimes I feel so cold, other times I feel so loving and warm. It's a new year, and I want to do things differently this year: to resolve my ambivalence, or at least be able to live with it; to be an upstanding person he can trust; and be someone who takes joy in things—though it may be too late to change. Obviously I am middle-aged. Middle-aged! I am just waiting out my days until my childbearing years have passed, and I can make good decisions again. Or perhaps make good decisions for the first time in my life.

Until then, there is nothing to do but get back into bed with him, where I know my body will hold his with gratitude. Could it really be that simple—just get out of my head and into my body? Get up close to his? I don't have faith in anything anymore. How am I ever going to get it? What two opposing things have to be brought together, in order to finally trust myself again?

~

When I got into bed, I cried in Miles's arms, then we slept. Sometimes I cry such hot tears just to feel how much I love him, and how tenderly I feel towards him, and how deeply I want him to be mine, and how awful it would be if he wasn't. If he left me, I would be heartbroken—it guts me to even think of it. But why should I think it? The way I have been acting, I feel possessed. It's really not me, but the worst, most insecure parts of me. I have to respond from the other parts. He said, *I will do anything to save this relationship except walk on eggshells around you*—but walking on eggshells is what I have been doing around him! He insists we only fight like this before my period, but I cannot be sure—I'm afraid to trust his interpretation of things. Even if it's true, I don't want to believe it. I don't know what to do if the problems aren't with him, but with me.

~

Waking this morning, I realized the extent to which I had been relying on Miles to make me happy. How great and huge my expectations for his behaviour have been. And how little responsibility I was taking for my own happiness. I see now how your life can only be what your insides are. Your life sits in your lap. I saw my life literally sitting there.

Teresa said that many of the relationships that are most solid and long-lasting are tumultuous at the start. I know that even with all our pain, I never want to be away from him for very long. I must love him, then. I must love what is. Love really does grow. A man becomes your family, and just as your family was chosen for you, so it seems as if the man who sticks around was birthed into your life from the very matter of the universe, no different from a howling baby. At least, that's the way it was for me the first time I saw Miles—like the universe stretched the way it does when a new life comes into being and is born.

On a certain level, you can never explain love. You never can know why. At a certain point, you have to accept the strangeness of love—the outsiderness of it compared to everything you have experienced before.

~

Now it seems you are at the point where being with Miles can't be debated. You have actually been in that place all along. Now that you have your mate in life, just move forward in your work and be glad for his existence. Don't expect Miles to fill in the hours for you, but be grateful that the hours are available for you to fill in as you like. He provides a constant stimulation for your desire, so you are not led into lostness, looking for other men. Our aloneness is so full, I never feel the need to have anyone else to fill up the empty spaces, for there are no empty spaces. And I so much love to be in his arms.

Sometimes we have so much anger towards each other. But we should be grateful to each other, for having helped each other—with however much pain—come to this new place, whatever this new place is. Instead, we hate each other. It's impossible to feel grateful.

Yet the man who doesn't leave, even when things are difficult—this reassures you. What is constancy? What is duration? My father's mother once told me with pride, *I kept my marriage.* When I asked her what the secret to a lasting marriage was, she said, *You eat crow.*

~

When Miles arrived home, after me yelling at him on the phone to come home, it was three in the morning and we hadn't spoken all day. All day it had just been awful, and the night before was awful too, and we just folded ourselves into each other's arms. I don't know if I slept or he slept or neither of us slept, but at a certain point he pulled up my nightie and began sucking my tits, then he went down on me, then he fucked me from behind, then he wanted to put his cock into my ass, but I didn't really want him to, yet I let him, but it felt bad, like I was shitting. I felt nervous and I told him this. *Relax, sweetie,* he said. I wondered why he wanted to go in my ass when he hadn't done it in so long. As soon as he got deep enough, I realized I didn't want to go any further or for him to come in my ass—I didn't want to give him that much right then—so I pulled away. He said, *I'm about to burst,* and he jerked himself off while I lay there and pulled up my nightie and fondled my tits. His eyes were closed at first, but when he opened them and saw what I was doing, he gave a great groan and he closed his eyes and came.

Later, when I went to wash myself off, I found a bit of red blood on the tissue, like a teardrop.

Mairon once said, *You can handle discomfort in your friendships; why can't you handle them in your romantic relationships?* She was pointing out that I wanted zero discomfort. She said, *You have to increase your tolerance for discomfort. You should be more courageous. What are you going to find if you run away? If you stay, maybe you'll see how strong you are—how much you can take, how it's okay to be hurt.*

Why do I listen to her? Because she's my friend? Yet all the women I know say similar things. And I say the same things back. We encourage the craziest behavior in each other. She said, *I think our marriage is harder for me than it is for him.*

Like soldiers nudging each other into battle, we nudge each other into relationships. *Stay there,* we say. *Don't run from the front lines.* That's what we are trying to convince each other of—that these are the front lines of life. If you run from the front lines, what good is your life? We encourage each other, *Go on—let yourself be maimed, annihilated, destroyed.*

These women are the voice of my conscience. They have no reason to lie. I have never met a woman who would not say the same thing, or who treats love lightly, like it is a game. We, the courageous, stand shoulder-to-shoulder. We cannot see our homeland. Maybe because we have no homeland anymore. We never thought we would last all the way to the end. But when the men started dying, and we all seemed so much lighter, freer, and more relaxed without them, then the children said, *They should have left our fathers such a long time ago—our stupid, old-fashioned, masochistic mothers.* But they grew up in peacetime. They didn't understand the thrill of war.

FOLLICULAR

Yesterday, at lunch at the dim sum place before Libby's wedding, there was a man from the wedding party who wanted to hold another guest's baby. He said (to no one in particular, standing up from the table) that he wished his wife would agree to another child—they already had two—but she said she didn't want another one. She wanted to return to work. He picked up the baby and carried it around the restaurant, as the baby opened her mouth wide with pleasure. She seemed glued to the man's arm—looked so secure. And the man seemed more solid with the baby in his arms than he had looked without. He suddenly turned into a different sort of man—a man with great value. The adults in the room meant nothing to him; he took the baby to the window—*It's a nice day outside!* he said. I saw him return to the baby three times during lunch, getting up from his chair and holding it close.

~

Miles and I were at Libby's wedding last night, which is where we fought. The bride and groom—their love was so believable, her standing there beside him in a beautiful wedding dress. I felt certain they were going to stay married and grow a life together— in a way that felt impossible for me. I could never have enough belief in the importance of my own marriage to pull off an expensive and beautiful wedding. I could never convince someone to pay that amount.

I know that many people accomplish this—not necessarily a happy union, but a beautiful and believable wedding—but it looked as impossible to me as flying to the moon. I saw the bride and groom as two cells whose marriage was contributing to the beauty of marriage in my mind—even though I knew that things had been hard for them, too. Yet last night, in the moment of their marrying, all their troubles seemed perfect because they only added to the triumph of the day. The most common human experiences—I have always longed for them so strongly. I cannot be critical. I am guileless before them, before all ceremony, or any ritual where humans make something symbolic together. I can't believe we have faith in anything at all.

Meanwhile, Miles and I fought, him glaring at me, me threatening to leave, both of us silent in the cab back home, wordless as we made our way to bed—me first, him hours later, after sitting up in the living room, playing video games for hours.

~

When Miles finally came to bed angry, I got very nervous—scared in my bowels—and we fought a bit more. Then he turned and pretended to go to sleep, and what came over me was the thought: *Stop playing this game—this is not a game. This is your life.*

I saw that in our fighting I had been playing a role, and I saw very quickly how much of every relationship, and just being a human, is playing a role. Then I felt a surge of joy and freedom, which must have been some form of nirvana, and which lasted less than a minute, but I saw how funny we all are, and what *I* am—not my behavior or my roles, but this burning light inside me that is laughing all the time. All of life looked so silly, for I realized what karma is: the playing of roles. You play roles, so keep yourself in certain situations, or get yourself into other predictable situations. Lying there in bed that moment, I could no longer remember what Miles and I were so upset about, but I saw what was the cause of so many problems—this pride, this ego, not wanting to lose face. It's as though we're these shells and the most important thing is to tend to them, and this tending makes them real—a real substance in the world—when actually they are nothing. How silly, stupid and petty we all are! Sitting here writing it down this morning, it doesn't feel like there is any way out, but in the place I inhabited last night, the way out wasn't an issue—I just felt extreme joy and peace at seeing what we put ourselves through for no reason at all.

I see how destabilizing it would be to act from this knowledge, rather than from our dramas—and I also see how radical love is, because it laughs at all the dramas, especially the drama of winning. Human life is a kind of myopia, everyone walking around, seeing only what's in front of them, or not even that—passing each other by, embroiled in our little dramas to such an extent that we miss out on everything; making big what is small. These desperate grasps at our own meaning!—when really our lives are meaningless. Our lives are meaningless, but Life is not—Life is hilarious and wonderful and brimming with joy. Life is pure freedom and it contains everything—even this dismal, grey human world.

~

Now I can hear him getting up—I have an angry man in the house with me. But why should I continue the fight? All this role-playing—it's real in the sense that it's actual and happening, but it isn't real in the sense that it's not the biggest story.

It all began when I told myself to take the situation more seriously—that *life is not a game*—for I realized that is how I was living it. Life is not a game, but we turn it into one. Will I win at being the perfect woman if I have children? Will I win at being an ideal woman if I do not? It seemed to me that the best thing in the world was to ride life—just be docile, accepting, happy and peaceful, and not make waves. I don't know why, but that seemed to me like the closest a human could approach to wisdom.

Then a person appeared to me who seemed to be in the middle of life—I saw them in a metropolis, kind of bright and floating through it. If someone called them for lunch, they went. They laughed often, and were easy—made no big issues about their choices or anything, for they knew that what they did didn't matter. Tightness, meanness, begrudging others, jealousy—it wasn't like the person who didn't have affairs was better than the person who did, but rather that the person who was open-hearted, humorous and warm, who made other people laugh, was better than the tightly mean and moralistic person. That is just the way it seemed.

I know that writing this down is a ridiculous act, the act of someone who has forgotten what she learned last night. Yet by writing it, I am bringing myself back to that same feeling of peace, happiness, lightness and joy. I can feel it returning now, even on this miserable day, when Miles and I are in the worst fight ever.

Yet that our lives are touched by, or made possible by, this absolutely incredible force—brighter than every human life put together—feels to me like the greatest gift. Life is persistent, and it doesn't flag in its loveliness, and it was a joy to have known it for just a moment—even if I can no longer feel it, because right now I'm too upset about other things—Miles and what we're going to do.

I think I am coming out of a very dark period, coming out of it as I speak. I just hesitated before asking a question I didn't want a *no* to. The question began *Is it my destiny to . . . ?* How much more careful I am now than I was last year, when I would have asked the coins any question at all. But now there are questions I don't want the answer to, and questions I don't feel it's right to ask.

Miles is out at dinner with his brother. What is one night in the long stretch of forever? Yet from the first moment it always seemed like we would never have enough time. And we don't. There will never be enough time, because I love him beyond time, bottomlessly, foreverly. Is that him now, stomping the snow from his boots? Is he going to come in and up to the second floor? No, no. It's the boy downstairs.

I don't want Miles to come home yet, bringing with him anxiety and chaos—but why must there be anxiety? Why must there be chaos? Why does my whole self pull towards him in frustrated desire, frustrated everything?

I just got out of the shower. The day is already dark, and the lamp is on beside the bed. I can feel the sadness in my heart of whatever was on the Internet, of all that I saw and read. There is no coming back from that sadness as the day turns dark. I want Miles to come home. I want him at home right now, but there is nothing I want to do with him here. I still have to wash the dishes. There is a tightness in my chest, the feeling of being an alien in my own life, no way home. I am sitting in bed with the empty-Internet feeling inside me, and there is nothing to do but feel empty—after that visit to absolutely nowhere at all. All the emptiness is inside me as night comes in—as the coldness comes in, and the sadness comes in, and the empty-hearted feeling comes in, and it comes in, and it comes in.

Last month, I began thinking about *the soul of time* as having something to do with cocoons. And I put a picture of a cocoon on my desktop—this one:

I recently learned that what happens in a cocoon is not that a caterpillar grows wings and turns into a butterfly. Rather, the caterpillar turns to mush. It disintegrates, and out of this mush, a new creature grows. Why does no one talk about the mush? Or about how, for any change at all to happen, we must, for some time, be nothing—be mush. That is where you are right now—in a state of mush. Right now your entire life is mush. But only if you don't try and escape it might you emerge one day as a butterfly. On the other hand, maybe you will not be a butterfly at all. Maybe you will become a caterpillar again. Or maybe you will always be mush.

~

I am sitting here, writing, in order to discover the simple secret of my existence—what sort of creature I am. And I am beginning to feel a widening in my chest. The aloneness of writing is coming to me again—the light, good feeling of being alone—the total aliveness of being alone.

Perhaps the cocoon I am meant to make is the cocoon that forms around me while writing. Then every day to go into it—into that cocoon of time and space, where everything stills, and my self becomes mush, and something new is formed. Inside this writing place, time and space are completely without form. Life has some defect of soul.

This is the me I most recognize as me—a self without fear, the self I most like to be with. It is not a me that is concerned with making choices or anything; it's a self without form, unimprisoned. The answer I gave when I was a child when someone asked me what sort of animal I wanted to be, always was, *turtle*. Maybe because a turtle is always at home? Even then, I always preferred to be at home. Perhaps I can carry my home on my back, if home is nothing but this cocoon, in which I can write and feel fine.

I want to be in this cocoon for as much of every day as possible—to remain within it as long as I can, and spend as much of my time as I can within it, and for it to be my shell, my protection against the world. No one can be in here with me. In here I feel no tears, I feel no emotion at all; no pleasure or pain.

But when I stick my head out of my shell to interact with people again, all of that disappears. The shell, the cocoon, the mush.

Somehow you think that in visiting the Internet, you can get the same pleasures you get in here. Why do you go there when you really want to come here? Thinking about the Internet, I can feel the tears coming back. That is my body materializing. That is my body coming back. It must mean that I'm no longer in my shell. My body materializes, speck by speck, and I'm no longer part of the void. I am a self again, no longer *no self*. I am no longer a paradoxical thing. The feeling of being on the Internet goes away in a few hours, like a common cold. That's what the Internet feels like—just a common cold—for it is common, and it is cold. Then don't go there at all. Or do. A little cold in your heart is not such a bad thing. But you do not need to be there every hour of the day. Besides, you should be working. I really need an infinity amount of time to work. Infinity sounds so dauntingly impossible!—but infinity can be accessed in moments like this one. It does not mean that to write this book, I need an infinity amount of time, but rather that I need to access infinity in time. Infinity is not a duration of time, it is a quality of time. I can reach it in moments like this one.

~

Waiting for Miles at the top of the stairs, I felt like the turtle I had wanted to be when I was a child. My head was stretched out of my shell, but I could feel the shell on my back, which I had created while I was writing.

And going to sleep, there was a bubble of happiness in me, or *I* was a bubble of happiness, a happiness I had not felt in such a long time. The bubble of happiness was my shell protecting me. And even lying in bed with Miles, I felt as if I could pull my head inside, and find my happiness there.

~

I spent four hours last night on the Internet, reading accounts of women who suffer from their moods in ways that feel so familiar—they want to run away from their life half the month, and the other half, life feels fine. Since tracking my periods, I see it's the same for me. But how can I tell whether there's something wrong with my life or not—when half the month all is roses, and the other half all is thorns? Which perspective should I trust? Is either one the truth?

Some women take anti-depressants for one week, or two weeks, before their periods come. Others take drugs the whole month. Some women are politically against drugs—but not, it seems, the ones who are suffering. At first, the ones whose relationships with partners and parents and children were in shambles didn't want to believe it—to give those around them the satisfaction of having identified their problem as PMS—especially because, while having PMS, they spent so much of the month hating these people.

I don't want to be like them, to need to be medicated in order to live—to admit there's something inside me that cannot be helped through will alone. But more than that, I can't live like this until menopause comes, spending half the month crumpled in tears. Half the month tearing everything down, and the other half building it up again. The idea makes me want to die.

Then, perhaps I will talk to my doctor—or try.

OVULATING

That sense, a long time ago, when we were fucking, his dick deep in me—I felt in the core of that darkness that he and I were, or would be, *ancestors*. I could understand us, our fighting, the complexity of things, when I understand us as ancestors.

With other men, I couldn't fall asleep beside them, or their cock felt strange inside me—just wrong. With Miles, everything fits so beautifully. The first time we fucked, I saw that my body always held itself back, even slightly, from other men. But my body rejects no part of his when we are naked together.

Perhaps life has stuck me with this man because it wants us to reproduce. Even if you think you don't want to, some magnet pulls you towards him, sticks you in an apartment with him, makes you think about marriage and children—tries to lead you there.

Perhaps you can resist the having of children, but you are still living with a man after all these years. And what are you doing with your mind? Is this the condition of being a woman—remaining obstinately in one place, because her body thinks that if she stays in one place long enough, she will have a child? She doesn't want a baby—but her body doesn't believe her. On some level, no one believes her. On some level, she doesn't even believe herself.

~

I have, for too long, relied on these coins. Shouldn't I be listening to my reason more?

yes

And shouldn't I be listening more closely to my instincts?

no

But it doesn't feel that way. It feels as though I *should* be listening to my instincts more. Or is that what has got me into trouble for so long?

no

Have I, in fact, not got into trouble?

no

No, I've got into trouble?

no

Difficulty in communicating?

no

Difficulty in understanding what is being communicated to me?

yes.

~

From now on, I want to follow my heart, do what is true for me. Instead of trusting myself, I've trusted people more. Why have I done this for so long? All the times I've listened to myself, has it ever been a mistake? Often, yes. But wasn't the freedom to make those mistakes greater than all the advice in the world?

Today I met Libby's baby, two months old. It was asleep in its blue bassinette. Libby told me that the moment she held her child in her arms, she thought, *I never need to meet anyone ever again.* Having met her child, it was enough for her. She felt finally filled up in a way that all the musicians, poets, painters, princes, filmmakers and phonies hadn't filled her up, who just left her hungrier than before.

Lying there in its bassinette, the baby seemed to be just waiting out its life in this magic web—this web that has caught another soul in it, to trap it here for so many years, then finally let it go again. The baby seemed to me a glimmering fish in a silvery net, a shining and throbbing soul; it didn't matter what it did with its life, just being here was the thing. I saw how our lives are not about action, are not about contemplation, they're just about being here, suspended in life's net—here for such a short time, glinting and glittering against the sun, lifted out of the ocean's depths to where everyone can see it, then plunged back in again—anonymous, gone.

Why would I brine a baby in my belly? What could ever persuade me to do such a hopeful thing—pull a glittering fish out of the deepest sea, to trap it in this beautiful life, a shimmering fish in a silvery net?

Libby said that I was a young soul, or must be, still discovering the world—she meant I was not an old enough soul to want to make a baby. But I said maybe I'm *too* old a soul to actually go through with it—to exhibit that hope, that patience, that care. Probably I'm just an old and stony mountain, hardened and crabby, who doesn't want any picnickers, any happy families, crawling all over its belly.

~

Libby has gone somewhere I can't—or won't—in raising a child that comes from her own body, which I am too cowardly, or know myself better than to let myself do. I'm incapable of doing it, or I don't want to—travel on the train to the underworld where she is going. She has gone to an underground that feels taboo for me, personally, and I am travelling to a place that feels taboo for her. It is the thinking about it, and the wondering about it, where she cannot go. It frightens her as much as to have a child scares me.

There are so many underworlds to travel to, not just one. There are so many taboos, and places forbidden to each one of us. I cannot understand how she can so blithely go into motherhood, without any hesitation at all—take on all that it requires, accept a new life into her life, which to me looks like death. But to her, my path seems like death, or is somehow forbidden for her to enter.

It seems we will have to travel alone. And we can't help but resent each other for this. Perhaps one day we can accompany each other again, but for now it feels impossible. She resents my freedom, the privilege of all my questioning, and I resent the privilege of her striding into a new life, without feeling the burden of all this questioning.

Of course, there are paths cut into any life, like in a forest of brambles you might find a clearing and proceed more easily down that path. It feels as natural for her to enter motherhood as it feels for me to entertain doubts. But my questions, for her, are no clearing in the woods, just deadly, choking brambles—just as motherhood feels to me like a garden of thorns that would prick me to death.

How hard it is to understand what the other has done—when it looks to me like she has been stolen, and when it looks to her like I have stalled. We both look so cowardly and so brave. The other one seems to have everything—and the other one seems to have nothing at all.

But we both have everything and nothing at all. We are both so cowardly and so brave. Neither one of us has more than the other, and neither one of us has less. It is so hard, I think, to see this: that our paths equal something the same; that having a child reflexively or not having one doubtfully are equal lives, the number of her life and the number of my life the same. That makes our hearts sink more than anything else, really, that the childless and the mothers are equivalent, but it must be so—that there is an exact equivalence and an equality, equal in emptiness and equal in fullness, equal in experiences had and equal in experiences lost, neither path better and neither path worse, neither more frightening or less riddled with fear.

This is the bland fact we cannot take. There has to be more to it than that, so we keep on piling up the scales, to see which side tips down just a little bit. Yet neither side tips any lower than its pair. They both hover at the same height in mid-air. I can't be any better than her, and she can't be any better than me. And this upsets us most of all.

I was in the grocery store when it began. I felt suddenly unafraid. I had never before realized that I had always been so afraid. The people around me doing their shopping seemed less menacing than before, when I would try to avoid them and avert my eyes. Now I could encounter them without worry, and I continued up and down the aisles, piling things into my arms. When I dropped my food onto the conveyor belt, the cashier looked up at me and said, *I see women do this all the time; men always take a basket. Women always make life harder for themselves than it needs to be.* I agreed. I had always thought I was saving time by not taking a basket. We laughed about this.

Walking home with my groceries in two white plastic bags, the world seemed bright and joyous. Then I realized it was the drugs kicking in. How was it possible that antidepressants were *legal?* Did half the country walk around feeling this way all the time—sparkling with ease and light?

That night, getting ready for bed, Miles sang a sweet and funny song he made up on the spot, about me, and I said to him, suspiciously, *Why are you being so nice to me?* Then I said, *Are you always this nice to me?* He said, *Yes.*

Over the next week, a tremendous rush of thoughts and feelings came to me—flooded past what had been the tall, thick wall between myself and the world, a wall that had prevented me from seeing, while giving me the impression that I was truly seeing. Everything had always been too loud, too close-up. Everything had always stung me too painfully. I had wanted to think about the world, but my anxieties forced me to think about myself—as if pressing into my face an injunction: *first you must solve this problem—the problem of your self.* But a rotating parade of non-problems is what it was—for example, when I would arrange to see someone for lunch in three days. Before, the *problem* of this would preoccupy me completely, and prevent me from thinking about anything else. Days lost to thinking about an appointment—and the shaking, jittering problem of living, which was so easily being whisked away with the drugs. Before, I was always scrambling to protect myself, but now I began to feel protected from the inside—as though I didn't have to plan ahead for every possible catastrophe, as though each cell in my body was cased in armour.

~

Before the drugs, sadness and anxiety was all I knew. Everyone says if you can whisk away your anxieties, you should. I had wanted to whisk them away, but I wanted to do it by old-fashioned means— means that didn't work—delving into my past, religion, spirituality, dreams—not by modern means, which are easy, and work. So far, no discernible side effects except a little clenching in the jaw, and the ability to sleep all day, if I want to.

Why should a modern person have to suffer twentieth-century problems? The problems of the psyche—a person living today should not have to suffer them! So I, like so many, am

electing not to. To untangle my past is to indulge in more fantasies, and I indulge in fantasy enough. Just give me some drugs!
At least for a few months, a year, ten years—just a break.
Besides, if a cure exists, isn't it dishonest not to take it? Isn't that
romanticism of the worst kind, almost cultish?

~

This is me returning. This is me coming back from an interior
I did not know was so intense. I didn't realize I'd been so separate from the world. The drugs seem to be working, that's all I
can say. The drugs really seem to be working. The fear in me,
the anxiety, is quelling because of these drugs. I have never felt
more strong, or so keenly aware of all the possibilities of my life.

~

Yet I fear I don't have the right to speak anymore, given these
drugs. I can't pretend I have come to any answers, or any great
wisdom. I think the drugs are the reason I am feeling less bad,
not something I realized. All those years, when I had been leaning on epiphanies to make me feel better, the feeling would last
for ten minutes, or a day, but it wouldn't really change anything.

Am I annoyed? Am I disappointed? A little bit, yes. I wanted
my own magic to get rid of the pain, but I suppose one's private
alchemy never works as well as drugs. Philosophy, psychol-
ogy, God, writing down one's dreams—they work as well as a
bloodletting, or leeches, or any medical intervention that does
not work.

What kind of story is it when a person goes down, down, down and down—but instead of breaking through and seeing the truth and ascending, they go down, then they take drugs, and then they go up? I don't know what kind of story it is.

Has this book, all along, just been evidence of my deep fear of everything, of all of life, and the things that matter to me most?

yes

Then is this *the book of the devil,* or *the devil's book*?

no

Is this *the book of the angel,* or *the angel's book*?

yes

Because I have been wrestling with an angel?

yes

And now I am not afraid?

yes

Of these same things will I ever again be afraid?

Early this morning, before leaving home to visit my mother in her new house out east, I dreamed I was lying on the lawn of a synagogue near where I grew up. Sitting on the other side of me was a woman who was professional, attentive, not very emotional. We were talking about my mother and how she wasn't around much when I was young. The woman, whose name was Tou Charin (I remembered this when I woke, because her name spelled *touch* if you put the first and last names together), couldn't understand why I had to have so many babysitters. She understood that my mother was a doctor and worked, but to her this didn't automatically mean that I had to have these substitute mothers. I explained that it wasn't so bad, it was nice—I said my babysitters were very warm. It was nice for me as a child. I remembered one taking me into her different neighborhood and into her brother's wonderful home. The different smells, the different furnishings, carpet on the stairs; I loved being there. I was getting choked up and distressed about it all. Finally, Tou Charin said she had to go, and she crossed the street, and went towards the subway. Hurriedly, I asked her for her email address. It was toucharin@gmail.com.

Watching her go, I realized that when I was a little girl I had made up a story: that a woman who works or cares deeply about her work can't also be a loving and attentive mother; that it was not *possible* to be both—that in order to explain my mother to myself, and to justify why she kept so much distance from me, it had to be because existentially one *couldn't* care about both one's work and one's child. So it wasn't my mother's fault. And it wasn't my fault, either.

~

I realized, while dreaming, that Tou Charin might be Charon, the ferryman to Hades, the land of the dead. So I pushed myself deeper into sleep and hurried across the busy, four-lane thoroughfare, pausing briefly on the grass-covered island as the traffic rushed past me on both sides, then I crossed the rest of the way and entered Eglinton West subway station through the glass doors, and rushed past the ticket booth. I went down the high escalator, onto the southbound platform.

As I was following Tou Charin, I wondered if she actually was the babysitter who lived with us, who held my hand when I was six years old. Travelling on the subway together, a strange man was following us, or I thought he was—staring at us in a way that made me feel scared. I remembered holding my babysitter's hand and telling her that I was afraid. She hugged me close and said, *You don't have to worry. I prayed for us before we left.* I had never before heard anyone say anything like this. My mother didn't believe in God, and my father had contempt for people who believed. So the fact that she had this faith, this *thing*—I wished I could have it, too. I so badly wanted to be religious, as I understood her to be. It was a superpower, really. But I also knew I would never have her faith—that I was already too old to have it, because I knew that God was not true. But for her it *was* true, or it was as true as it needed to be, because she wasn't scared.

~

At the bottom of the escalator, I found Tou Charin standing there. I went over and stood beside her.

I noticed that on the opposite platform, among the people waiting for the train, were two large dogs. I had seen them running into the station when I entered, bounding in large, wide loops, then down the stairs. After a couple of minutes, the train pulled in. The doors opened. When the doors closed and the train left, only one dog remained on the platform, looking around for its friend.

I watched that dog, worried for it, and sad. It was distressed about its missing friend, and it looked anxiously down the platform. Then my train arrived. I realized I hadn't paid the fare, but had just slipped by the conductor's booth upstairs.

How much is it? I asked Tou Charin.

Three coins, she said.

I hesitated a moment, then gave them to her, and got on.

In the train, I felt I was being borne away, even farther from my mother friends and from Libby, like a dog who stepped onto a train going in the wrong direction from its companions, not realizing what it had done, not knowing what it meant.

My mother opened her front door with a proud, sweet smile. She led me through her house, which had once been a barn, but which had been renovated to look like any ordinary, middle-class home. She admitted she rarely left it, for even in her retirement she is somehow still working. She didn't mind. *I used to worry that I was missing out on all the things happening in the world,* she said.

I worry about that, too.

But nothing is happening in the world. Don't worry, she told me. *You're not missing out on anything.*

~

We sat and talked in armchairs that were covered in rich velvet the color of pomegranates. And the walls were painted a soft yellow. The wood trim was stained walnut, and there were tchotchkes everywhere—a porcelain bear holding a dish sponge, bear magnets on the stove, and other bears, stuffed and sweet, on the cabinets and the windowsills.

Her study on the second floor was lined with shelves, and on them were books about mythology, astronomy and anatomy—books that had something real inside them, which corresponded not only to the human world, but to the world of nature. They had something in them of the grasses and shrubs that were stirring on the hills just outside her home, and something of the waves lashing onto the rocks; something of the saltiness of the sea air, which rose up against the cliff's edges, where the sheep grazed in pastures near where she lived.

Her study had a Persian rug covering the floor and more soft chairs. In the study, she opened a door that I thought would lead into another room, but I was startled to see the door open onto the vast and cavernous barn that her house had been built up from. Light poked down through the slats, and there were angled and rotted boards, and dust and cobwebs and darkness everywhere. I felt dizzy—like she was showing me her unconscious, the basement of her mind. How far away can we get from our mind's darkest structures? It seemed to me like her living space would never be far enough from her deepest self— it would always be so close, right there, behind a closed door. And that this was the same for all of us—one could furnish the darkness and put in couches and try to live happily there, but just open the door and you would drop down into the darkest shadows.

~

Late one night, after my mother was asleep, I wrote my former Classics professor and I asked her about the words *tou charin*, which had remained in my mind. Earlier, expecting nothing, I had search for the words online, and found they appeared in Aristophanes' play *The Frogs*. So I asked her if she could explain it to me—what *tou charin* meant. Her reply came the next day:

In English we'd pronounce "tou charin" as "to karin" with a hard *k* and sounding like the woman's name Karen. *Charin* is a very close cognate to *Charon*, the ferryman of Hades who crosses souls over the river Styx.

On its own, *charin* could mean *grace, favor, an act of kindness,* but with the added *tou* it becomes a phrase, like *por favor* in Spanish. *Charis* appears in the phrase, *For her pleasure. For talking's sake. For the sake of my flesh. An offering in consequence of a vow. Tou Charin* might mean *On account of, for the sake of, because of, by reason of, in favor of, for the pleasure of—this.*

So Dionysus says, *"I came down [to Hades] for a poet."*

"For what reason?" (tou charin)

Some sources of the play have Dionysus asking himself this question rhetorically. Others have Heracles asking it of him directly. So either Dionysus is asking himself, *For what reason do I do this (act of kindness)?*—meaning his descent into Hades. Or else, in the voice of Heracles, *Why do you make this descent?*

In Greek literature, a descent into Hades always has something of a dreamlike quality, Hades and dreams being very much linked. And the reason Dionysus gives for the descent is to bring back an old, great Tragedian. Making him return to the living world of people would be a succor to the failing Athenians in their time of need.

~

Over the next few days, my mother drove me through her tiny village, but the entire time I felt half-asleep. I apologized to her for being so tired. She wanted to have lunch with me by a canal, where two swans floated under a wooden bridge, but I kept yawning, and I was desperate to get back to the house and sleep. We finally returned, and I napped on the blow-up mattress, which I blew up by myself.

In my dream, I saw before me a mirror, and I knew I had to get beyond the mirror—so summoning all my strength, and knowing it required a huge act of faith, I leapt through it. Then I found myself falling down a tubal organ—a vagina or a trachea. As I was falling, I told myself to fall with abandon, because I knew I was in a dream, so I could not get hurt, and I wanted to go even deeper into my psyche, which I knew is what the falling represented. When I landed at the bottom, I found myself in the dank basement of my childhood home; there was a photo album on the floor, and I began to look through it. I found a photograph of my mother's face, with the expression she had always worn when I was a child: full of mistrust, unhappiness and distance. Then I turned the page and saw a close-up of another face—smiling, and full of big, white teeth and happy eyes. When I woke up on the floor—the mattress having sunk down—I felt different, as though I could choose the happiness of that smiling face, or the unhappiness of my mother. Not everything had to be so heavy all the time. But how deep inside me my mother's face was! How it lay in the basement, the unfinished barn, of my soul—so close, right there.

~

It happened so often during my childhood that our family would be sitting at the kitchen table, eating dinner. Then, without any warning, my mother would suddenly be crying, and she would get up and hurry off to the bedroom, in tears. Many times I followed her, but she would not open the door, would tell me to go away—she was unwilling to see me or be comforted.

After a while, I stopped following her. We would remain at the table, and just continue talking as though nothing had happened.

~

I rose from my nap and went into the kitchen, and my mother and I sat at the table and drank the coffee she had been boiling on the stove. She said, *Your father said to me on the phone last week that maybe it's a good thing we don't have grandchildren—given the horrible state of the environment, and what the world will be like in fifty years.*

The intimacy of my mother and father belonging to the same fate—*maybe it's good 'we' don't have grandchildren*—made me feel strange, like I was a young child: sheepishly responsible for binding my parents together in an endless experience of parenthood.

~

On the following day, sitting on the cliffs alone, overlooking the sea, I had brought my notebook with me, but with the beauty that surrounded me, I could not write. Nature's beauty could not be captured, nor could anything I write equal its grandeur. When I returned to the farmhouse after hurrying down the hill, I entered my mother's kitchen and saw that she had put out sliced fruit, and had turned on the radio and was listening to a show. I showered and got changed, and when I returned to the kitchen, she was preparing a dish from a cookbook for dinner, with tomatoes and balsamic vinegar, and the salmon we had picked up earlier from the fishmonger in town. When I was growing up, she had only ever made schnitzel.

My mother told me about her plans to renovate the rest of the barn. She wanted to expand it, to make an apartment for herself on the main floor with a bedroom and a tub, so she would not have to climb the stairs when she *became ancient*.

Since my girlhood, I had been cautious about allowing myself to imagine the beauty of being a woman alone in a house by the sea. Yet now I saw the beauty my life could become.

~

The next morning, I peered into the cabinet while brushing my teeth, and saw a bottle of blue-and-yellow pills behind the mirrored glass, nestled beside the mouthwash, some eye shadow, and several frayed and yellowing toothbrushes. My mother's name was on the label.

When I entered the living room with the bottle and asked her about the drugs, she admitted that she had taken them on and off these last few years. It suddenly made sense: I felt I could identify any memory of my mother as either being on the drugs, or off them. On them, she is more cheerful, warm and delightful. Off them, she is sad and withdrawn, but more poignant in some ways—a towering figure with tremendous power.

~

When my mother came to my room to say goodnight, I told her I loved her, and although I have said this many times before, this time she said, with a funny smile on her face, *I am surprised you love me, when I neglected you so much.* She said that before the divorce, she was focused on keeping the marriage together, not on loving her *kiddies.* She went on, *I paid attention to the wrong things.* I saw what a different person she would have been if we had been her focus, but it seemed strange that it was a *choice.* I mean that *choice* seemed like the wrong word for something that to me was always just the way it was, and couldn't possibly have been any different.

Right before my mother left the room, she spoke, with some confusion, about women who say that raising kids is the most important thing in their life. I asked her if motherhood had been the most important part of her life, and she blushed and said, *No*—at the very same moment that I interrupted her and said, *You don't have to answer. I was there.*

~

The surprise my mother delivered to me when we sat on her couch, the day before I left—I told her that my father had been angry at her since their last interaction, and told her about my brother's anger, too. Instead of self-pityingly criticizing herself, or making frantic plans to win their love back, as I was used to her doing, she said, *So what? I'm not going to go and hang myself.*

What does that mean? I said. I had never heard her say anything like that before.

She said she was going to enjoy her life despite their anger at her—she wasn't going to go and kill herself because her ex-husband and son were upset at her for reasons of their own.

When she said this—*So what? I'm not going to go and hang myself*—it did something inside me. If she is not going to hang herself, then neither am I—not for any reason at all. Do you ever feel like you cannot grow beyond your mother? So it's wonderful when your mother climbs one step higher on the ladder from where she had been standing before.

I flew south to meet Miles at a seaside town, where we would be joining his daughter and her mother. It was the town they had named their daughter after. We stayed in a beachside hotel in two rooms, and spent three days on the sand. It was an experiment, a hopeful one: the first time the four of us had ever been away together.

It was particularly hot on the second day, and Miles and his daughter went down the shore to get ice cream for everyone. Her mother and I turned to each other while lying on the beach towels and said, *Do you want to go into the ocean? Yes.*

Twenty minutes later, they returned from the concession stand with ice creams in each of their hands. Then Miles's daughter stepped away from him and went to stand by the shore. Holding the ice creams, she watched us—her mother and me—bobbing far in the waves. Seeing her seeing us swimming together was perhaps one of the most wonderful moments of my life.

Here I am—back in my apartment that is filled with books. The lonely fill up their lives with books. I don't live in nature. I don't live in culture. I don't live in my relationships. I live in books. What good can all the books of the world be, penned by the loneliest men who ever lived?

Tonight, neither Miles nor I could sleep, so he pulled off my pajamas and went down on me till I came, then we fucked, then I sucked him off and he came loudly, crying out into a pillow. Then we lay there holding each other, but I couldn't sleep from the jet lag, so I came into this room and read sixty pages of a book, then I listened to the rain fall hard outside the window, with just one lamp on, and drank my hot chocolate. After that was done, I looked through the magazines in the pile on the sideboard, and determined to throw some of them out today.

This morning, I feared I might be pregnant. I felt it so strongly: *But I don't want a child!* Walking home from the pharmacy, with the sunlight streaming down on me, and crossing into the park where the children played, I took the morning-after pill.

~

A measure of impatience, a bad feeling on the walk, too many sunflowers lining the edge of the lawn, not enough sun for everyone, the distribution of love wholly unequal, the sense that one is being depended on, the sense that one is failing. The feeling that there is little in life left to strive for; something having been accomplished, not much left to do. A feeling of uselessness, of the end of the world coming, of other people's lives having no purpose, of all of us doing whatever we feel like, no collective direction in which we're all taking part. And another dark shadow on a dark lawn: the fact that for a woman of curiosity, no decision will ever feel like the right one. In both, too much is missing.

What can I say, except: I forgive myself for every time I neglected to take a risk, for all the narrowings and winnowings of my life. I understand that fear beckons to a person as much as possibility does, and even more strongly.

~

I should have known all along that this would happen. All the times I contemplated children, I felt a giddiness and wobbliness that are nothing like the commitments I've made that come from a deeper, more solid place. Those commitments feel dark, unfantastical, mixed up equally with the good and the bad. But the thought of having children always made me feel dizzy, or as elated as sucking helium, like all the things I've rushed into, and just as impulsively, left.

Coming back from the bank today, an old man in his garage did not look at me, even though I passed close by. It made me glad, for I never much enjoyed being looked at anyway. How freeing to escape the grip of that world, and move into another realm entirely—one not so dominated by men's desires, but to breeze past their desires. Only when a woman is no longer attractive to men, can she be left alone for enough moments to actually think.

~

I feel so relieved that it has passed—like a storm passing over my soul. The storm has passed and the clouds have given way to a brighter day, lighting up the world all around me. I can see it again—what I saw before, my whole life long—how far out in all directions life can go. Before, when the thought of having a child was near, I couldn't imagine any distance or depth to a life without one. It felt like emptiness, like boredom, like poverty— like all the things I loved would never be enough, would never make up for this lack; that life would always have a lacking.

But now that I am older, my oldness makes me not want them. My life is not a speculative life, or a blueprint for a future life. It's just my life. This oldness is a good feeling—a feeling of nothing more to be decided. What happens now will be something other than the strain of making a decision, or the stress of fighting with nature, trying to assert what is true for me in the face of what it wants.

I experience biology's forgetting about me as an immense relief, as a sort of bliss. If you do not have a child, at a certain age you become your own child. You start life all over again, this time with yourself. And what will I do with all this time? But time is not what you do something with—time does something with you.

Admit it when you have waited too late, when the time for something is passed. It can be too late not only for biological reasons, but because the moment has honestly passed. When the sun has set, the meal you eat cannot be called breakfast. I'm in the afternoon of my life. The time for children is breakfast.

~

I never thought that by the time I came to this part, I would be so old—that what would happen was simply aging, time doing its work, playing on its instrument—me. It's all so frighteningly simple, the end to all this questioning—but also, unexpected. I wondered about children intensely for so long, but now that I am getting older, I am thinking about it less and less—with some relief, a bit of distress, but mostly no sentiment at all.

What I don't realize fully is that I'm actually at the end of my childbearing years, which means that nobody is interested in hearing me ask the questions I most fear, long after the questioning entirely makes sense. I can't completely admit it to myself—that the time for deciding has passed. I can't say it outright, or accept that I have missed my chance, or that I did everything in my power to miss it—that I *wanted* to miss my chance. That it was a chance I never wanted, yet I felt obliged to consider it—to consider it until the very last second—before finally turning away.

It's fair to say I'm missing out on something—but also that I might prefer to miss out.

I held fast against the wave that tried to sweep me into its slumber—the slumber that makes babies—for it's certainly a kind of slumber to do what nature wants. To have avoided its grasp feels as blissful and intimate as having a child, but the opposite of a child, in how what I've won can hardly be seen.

I love the people who exist already, and there are so many books to read, and so much silence to inhabit. I don't have to live every possible life, or to experience that particular love. I know I cannot hide from life; that life will give me experiences no matter what I choose. Not having a child is no escape from life, for life will always put me in situations, and show me new things, and take me to darknesses I wouldn't choose to see, and all sorts of treasures of knowledge I cannot comprehend.

~

When I was a child, and I imagined a future life with children, I always wound up at the thought that one day I would be an orphan. Part of me looked forward to this time, as though in the moment both my parents had died, I would become like a star in the sky, beautifully and profoundly alone. But if I had children, I would never be that shining thing, enveloped by a darkness, completely untouched.

Then didn't I know it all along—that a baby would never come from between my legs? I think I knew it from a very young age—that it could not happen, and never would. My body has always experienced the idea of having a child as an absurdity and an abomination. I never thought I would die leaving a child from my body behind. If I had asked myself that question, thinking about my deathbed, I really would have known. I should have looked at my deathbed, not at the maternity ward. For as inconceivable as it is—a child from my womb—even more inconceivable is a child mourning me once I'm gone. I should have looked at it backwards.

Last night, lying in bed, Miles said to me,

Nobody looks at a childless gay couple and thinks their life must lack meaning or depth or substance because they didn't have kids. No one looks at a couple of guys who have been together forever, love each other, are happy in their work, have chosen not to have kids, are probably still fucking, and pities them; or thinks that down deep inside they must know they're living a trivial and callow life because they're not fathers. Nobody thinks that! The idea of it is ridiculous! Or take a lesbian couple who could have had kids if they wished to, but chose not to for whatever reason. Now they're in their fifties or sixties, one of these glorious couples you see around, with that ease and assuredness they have, like they don't need any favours from anybody. Who looks at them and thinks they must be nurturing this bottomless regret and longing in their souls because they're not mothers? Nobody! It would be offensive to suggest, not to mention stupid. It's only straight couples people have these feelings about—how empty their lives must be. No, actually, it's not even the man—people look at him like he got away with something. It's just the woman—the woman who doesn't have a child is looked at with the same aversion and reproach as a grown man who doesn't have a job. Like she has something to apologize for. Like she's not entitled to pride.

~

I realized then that in my darkest moments, I had been afraid that Miles didn't respect women, but now I wondered if his not needing me to be a mother revealed a deeper respect for me and for women than even I had—with my endless searching deep inside to find a desire to be a mother, hoping I'd discover that self there, thinking that if only I looked long enough, I could scare her out from her hiding place and finally be *her*.

In my moments of greatest paranoia and hurt, I thought he must see something wrong with me if he did not want to use me for having a child. Why couldn't I consider that he valued me simply for myself? He was not asking to use me for anything. How had I taken this as a rejection of me as a woman? He wanted to be with me for *me*, while I had wanted him to value me as a means of continuing himself through me. It was my mind that was warped, not his. He had seen me as a full and final person, and this had hurt my feelings and made me feel suspicious.

I wondered at myself angrily, so many times, *Why did you fall in love with a man—and remain with him through your thirties—who is so hard to have a baby with?* But now that question seems to answer itself: because I wanted to be with a man who would not make it easy for me to have my own baby, because I didn't really want one—just as some women choose a partner in the opposite way, as someone to have children with.

Walking through the neighborhood, the grasses are pushing up through the sidewalk, but they all had their start beneath the ground. So maybe it's okay that for a very long time, I have also been underground. The thickest tree was once the thinnest. What very strong thing in nature did not start off as weak? If up until now I have been weak, that does not mean I will never be strong.

~

I feel a new giddiness and wonder that I managed to pass through my childbearing years without bearing a child. It really feels like a miracle, like something I always set out to do, but had no faith that I would ever achieve. I didn't know whether I would make it—but now there is relief inside.

Anything could happen now. I feel I have lived through the trickiest part of my fate. And how much gratitude I have towards Miles, for without him I might never have arrived in this place.

~

In the early days of writing this book, I thought it would be a trick: that I would write it and it would tell me whether I wanted to have a child. You think you are creating a trick with your art, but your art ends up tricking you. It made me write it and write it for years—the answer like something I could almost reach, tantalizingly there—the promise of an answer just around the corner, maybe in the next day's writing. But that day never came. But the hope that it would lead me past the ages of thirty-six, thirty-seven, thirty-eight, and thirty-nine—and in a few months I will be forty.

Even a few months ago, I felt like I had to finish this book—to have it done by the end of this year; imagining this book was the single thing I had to do before having a baby. But last night I imagined *not* racing to finish this book; not giving myself only two more months with it, but ten months, or a year, or two years, or ten. And this felt a million times more nurturing than rushing to finish it in time to have a baby; a million times more loving and true.

Taking the knife that sat in front of my mirror, I hold it in my hands like my mother held a scalpel in that photograph of her from medical school. A corpse lies on a table before her, and she stands with three other women doctors. They seem to be having such a good time. I can't believe my mother is wearing her watch, and her green-and-gold ring.

Taking the knife to slice it all open, what have I found in my autopsy of a body laid upon the page? And that fortune teller who I met in New York: I wondered if what she said was true. She said my maiden name would be remembered, and my married name would be, too.

She said that Miles and I would have two girls, and that we

would stay together until I died. She also said I had pre-cancerous cells in my womb. But it was my grandmother, Magda, who gave birth to two daughters. It was she who remained with her husband until she died, and she who had pre-cancerous—and finally cancerous—cells in her womb. And it was she who had a married name and a maiden name while I only have this one name.

If it is true what the fortune teller said—that three generations of women in my family were cursed—then my great-grandmother was surely more cursed than me. She was so poor that she lived in a house with dirt floors, and she and her husband died young of the flu, because they could not afford the medicine or care, leaving behind four children. It was she whose orphaned children were taken to Auschwitz, and one of them killed in the camps. How exactly have I been cursed? I haven't been. I have always had luck at my feet, through no good works of my own.

Yet my grandmother never wrote a book, so when the fortune teller was talking about a book, she must have been talking about this one. And I do think she was speaking about me when she said, of a man, *Your life is safe in his hands.*

My mother gave me the middle name Magdalen. She put her mother inside me. So perhaps the fortune teller was speaking both to me, and to the Magdalen inside of me.

~

I think I used my ordinary, humble sadness with Miles to access a bigger sadness that wasn't mine. All the times I thought I was upset about Miles, I think I made the sadness bigger, made it wider so I could tunnel inside. I used our fights to make the tears come—needed the pain to touch a sadness that went so far back and deep inside, to try to heal it there.

Then I remembered how the tarot reader said, *There is a way of saying, Could you please send that ball of pain back where it belongs, if it isn't mine? Actually say, 'I'm sending this back now. And please send it back in the most healed and loving form it can go. But I don't want it, it's not welcome, and it's not helping me.'*

I think this book is the most healed and loving form I can make. Then should I send this book across the ocean to where my grandmother is buried—give it to the worms and bugs who live in the soil of my grandmother's grave? But why do they deserve this sadness? Maybe I'll just scatter it like ash in the world—as if publishing a book is like scattering ashes from an urn—in the sea, in the forest, in a city, anywhere.

~

Maybe I will take this book to my mother's house. I will knock on her door and go up to her and say, *It's here. On the page. Your mother's sadness, and your sadness, and mine. Although not all of the reasons. I don't know all of the reasons.*

As she reads through it, I'll stand there and wonder: Do you think with our lives we validated your mother? Do you think we helped her at all? Did we do our job? Can her life be said to be worth what you thought it was worth? Is this the first thing we have ever done together? You carried the nightmares, and I carried them, too. Can we put them down now? In putting down this book, will you put your sadness down? Put down whatever remains of your task, and finally rest satisfied?

Maybe she will say, *It's okay that you don't know all of the reasons. When I diagnose a cancer, I don't need to say the reasons. I'm just asked whether it's malignant or benign.*

Then these tears, I will say, *this pain, this sadness, this tumour-like growth. In your professional opinion, is it malignant or benign?*

I've looked it over carefully—and my opinion is that it's benign. My suggestion is not to operate. There are more dangers associated with taking it out than leaving it inside.

I was in a small town, giving a reading at a literary festival, several hours' drive from home. I finished writing these pages, and then, with a fear I didn't completely understand, and yet at the same time which I understood well, I sent these pages off to my mother. I asked her to please read them, and let me know whether she would rather I use her mother's maiden name, Becker, or her married name, Waldner. Without thinking about it anymore, I sent them off, and a great pleasure filled me.

~

I went out to explore the area for the first time since I arrived. I left the apartment in the little house where I was staying, and walked down Lighthouse Street to where a cliff overlooked the bay, and everything was green and wet. It had been raining all day, but now the rain had stopped. After walking along the cliff's edge, I discovered some wooden steps leading down—all the way, I supposed, to the beach. I was wearing white sneakers, a white nightgown, and a grey sweatshirt—a little underdressed for the weather. I went down five or six steps before my feet slipped out from under me and I fell down the whole flight, landing roughly as the back of my shins knocked again and again against the wooden steps which were cut into the hill. I jumped up quickly, like an animal spooked, and hobbled back up the hill, going quickly across the grassy field back towards the street. Strolling past me was an elderly couple. They were heading to the cliff's edge to watch the sunset, and even though it was almost nine at night, only a touch of redness could be seen against the clouds which lined the edge of the horizon. The woman saw the bruises appearing on my legs, and she said, *That looks bad—you should put some Arnica on that.* We stood there, the three of us, and watched the end of the sunset. The man said, *twenty miles down, and thirty kilometers across, there is the largest bed of salt in the country—it's a salt mine.* The woman and I hadn't known this. After the couple walked off, I remained in the grassy field, and watched the sky grow dark. All I wanted was to stay there through the night, just fall asleep in the grass, and wake with the dew in the morning.

~

When morning arrived, I sat up in bed in the little house where I was staying, and reached over to the side table, on which rested my phone. There was an email from my mother, which had arrived ten minutes before, just as I was stirring awake. I pulled it close and read her message.

Subject line: *It's magical!*

My mother was the person I loved the most, was the most important person in my life for the longest time.

When I was pregnant with you, it never occurred to me that I would have a son. I lost my mother. I had to have a daughter to make the Universe perfect again.

You will be soon forty years old and she died about forty years ago. You never knew her, and you are the one who will make her alive forever.

It is magical! And yes, the Universe is back to perfect.

Thank you, Sweetheart. I love you very much.

Then I named this wrestling place Motherhood, for here is where I saw God face-to-face, and yet my life was spared.